The Nest

Sarojini Sahoo

Translated by
Tapan K Panda

BLACK EAGLE BOOKS
Dublin, USA | Bhubaneswar, India

Black Eagle Books
  USA address:
  7464 Wisdom Lane
  Dublin, OH 43016

India address:
E/312, Trident Galaxy, Kalinga Nagar,
Bhubaneswar-751003, Odisha, India

E-mail: info@blackeaglebooks.org
Website: www.blackeaglebooks.org

First International Edition Published by
Black Eagle Books, 2023

THE NEST
by **Sarojini Sahoo**
Translated by **Dr. Tapan K Panda**

Cover: **Raghunath Thakur**
Interior Design: Ezy's Publication

ISBN- 978-1-64560-396-2 (Paperback)
Library of Congress Control Number: 2023938808

Printed in the United States of America

The novel titled *Pakhibaasa,* in Odia Language, establishes a firm balance between becoming and being. Sarojini's language as well as style is forceful and dignified. The whole novel is sharp and sure in its judgement It moves with the ease and precision as the writer is in perfect possession of her materials.

The Nest is a true reflection of the struggle, hope and dreams of the protagonist in a global language.

Sadananda Tripathy
Author, 'Kathaa Subhe Lathaa Rahijae' and 'Ranganatha Ghadei '

Sarojini Sahoo is one of the finest story tellers of our times. She is predominantly known as a first-generation feminist in modern Odia literature. Contrary to this tag, this work reveals her art and craft in weaving the story of a Dalit family. She has lived in Western Odisha for a long span, and it seems she has met all the characters of this novel, Antara and his three sons and only daughter. On the background flows a symbolic representation of a story from Bhagavata. The story reflects how the dreams of a poor and Dalit family have been shattered into pieces. Sarojini Sahoo ' s artistry in description- sharp, short, yet heart touching makes it a masterpiece.

The Nest in English is for the wider audience and am sure will take the issues and challenges of downtrodden reflected in the original into newer heights and global audience.

Hiranmayee Mishra
Author, 'Red Wine Ra Raati' and 'Kalijai O Anyanya Galpa'

In *"Pakhibaasa"* , Sarojini Sahoo weaves the story of a tribal family that goes through various turmoil and horrible instances. A very realistic portray of poverty, uncertainty, helplessness and revolutionary activities, this multi layered novel is sure to agitate the reader, probing them to think.

Dr Tapan Panda has given justice to this engaging narrative, translating the emotion and essence that Western Odisha holds through the translated version *"The Nest"*.

Chirashree Indrasingh
Author, 'Bengabati Katha' and 'Kimbhira Desha'

Beautiful story of every parent who want to see their kids successful but are not able to get the things right for them. *The Nest* will surely give you goosebumps as you will proceed with the turmoil of a Satnemi and his family...

Prachi Garg
Author, 'Kakori' and 'Super Women'

Dedicated to all the Satnemis of the World

Preface

Pakhibaasa (published in English as The Nest) is my all-time favourite novel. It took me almost three years to write this short novel. I regularly received a magazine named 'Dernaa' published in western Odisha at my Rampur Colliery address. I don't recall the year and month; maybe it was two thousand six or seven; with my handholding, this magazine moved into another world. The magazine published many fact-based articles about Dalits (the downtrodden people). The magazine had a solid and intense voice against the upper-class atrocities and *Manu Samhita*. I used to read every page of that magazine in one go. I was deeply influenced by the writings of *Bijay Sahis* during those days. Though it was a small piece, it impacted me immensely. I travelled to many places to collect information about *Satnemis*.

Once I was in a *Satnemi* Slum near Rampur. I could see people carrying a woman in a rope-webbed cot used as a carrier. This was the first time I had seen such a picture. Since it was something new for me, it was apparent that I was curious, but no one in the family had any worries! There was a strange emptiness in their eyes. I could see an elderly man or woman at everybody's door front. As if the youth had vanished from the village. I could learn many things during my interaction. I could learn about the secrets behind their disappearance.

I started working on the novel "*Pakhibaasa (The Nest)*" during the summer vacation of 2005. For some unknown reason, I didn't like the writing even after completing almost twenty to twenty-five pages. Writing stopped then and there. Then I wrote the novel '*Gambhir Ghara' (The Dark Abode)*, which generated many controversies. The plotline was based on social media-based pseudo-relationships and Indo- Pak issues. Though *Gambhiri Ghara* (The Dark Abode) was at its peak for being one of the controversial novels, my mind was still stuck at *Pakhibaasa (The Nest)*. I rewrote the novel after six to eight months. During those days, there was news on the national channel about the failure of a young man from a tribal hamlet drawing Idital paintings, who was sent to Japan by Missionaries for an art exhibition in returning to the homeland. The pregnant wife at home was running pillar to post, seeking the government's help to return her husband. From there, Sannyasi's character came into existence. After that, I didn't stop, and the novel pulled me in.

In almost all my novels, I have some element of poetry. I have adopted the tragic episode of the dove couple from the eleventh chapter *(Skanda)* and eighth sub-chapter *(Adhyaya)* of *Bhagavat*. The novel draws its name from this adoption. I have also occasionally used the Sambalpuri dialect in the book.

While writing this novel, I don't know how far I have successfully described their agony and suffering. Still, I am convinced that this could have been more meaningful if one of these people had attempted this novel. Before its English edition, Yas Publications published this novel in Hindi, Samaya Prakashan in Bengali from Dhaka. After being serialized in a Kannada magazine, it has been published in Kannada. I thank poet Tapan K Panda for showing interest in translating the novel into English. I hope the book will be appreciated by a wider audience. Then only the hard work of both myself and Tapan will be fruitful.

Sarojini Sahoo

Translator's Note

M s Sarojini Sahoo is an established name in Indian literature. She is equally famous for her feministic outlook and bluntness in keeping her views above the women-centric reservations. Well known for her thoughts on 'liberal woman' in Odia literature, many of her short story collections and novels have been translated and published in different Indian languages. *Pakhibaasa* (The Nest) is her sixth novel.

The novel *Pakhibaasa* (The Nest) is centred around the landscape of western Odisha (the undivided districts of Koraput, Kalahandi, and Sonepur). This novel entails the heartbreaking story of the life of animal bone gatherer *Chamaar* cast people (*Satnemis*) who live below the poverty line. This novel describes the naked truth of the disintegration of a happy family under adverse social conditions. Towards the end of the novel, losing everything, both the protagonists have become indigent. Their family is broken. Whatever we call a household is filled with an endless void. Both lives are drooping in old age, grief, and loneliness. There is no escape from this. The novel is only a shrieking of humanity.

Antaraa, the novel's hero, has always dreamt of flying above his situation and environment. So, he has named his children a sequence as Collector, Doctor, Lawyer and *Paraba* for his only daughter. None of his children could become doctors, collectors, or lawyers; the first son leaves for an unreachable distance from home after converting to Christianity. The doctor moves as a bonded labour, and Okil eventually turns into a Naxal and gets killed. The smell of a fistful of boiled white rice forces the only daughter Parabaa to accept prostitution in Raipur.

Antaraa's traditional occupation is of a bone collector, where he sells them for a living. On a conscious level, he is no less than a monk. Antaraa lives a spiritual life at a personal level and feels happy by organizing discourses on *Bhagavat* for the villagers. Though reading and delivering sermons on *Bhagavat* is entirely opposite to his livelihood, one can experience the psychic elevation of *Antaraa* is evident in the *Pakhibaasa (The Nest)* novel. The novelist has added the episode of a dove couple from the eleventh chapter and eighth sub-chapter of *Bhagavat.* Both the doves and men have their own suffering under 'the illusion', yet the author wishes to illustrate that there is no difference between the animals.

'*Pakhibaasa'* is a poem by itself that emerged within the soul. It's a poem of revolt. This poem of failed anger makes the reader reach remotely settled villages like Kisinda, Sidingagudaa, and Sinpali - far away from the glittering capital. It makes the reader arrive at a different India.

I would like to thank Ms Sarojini Sahoo for allowing me to work on her favourite novel and make it available for a larger global audience and for trusting me to do the translation.

While working on the portions from *Bhagavat* for the episode on Doves, my friend, eminent storyteller, and poet Ms Chirashree Indrasingh's daughter Madhur Singh Pradhan helped me to bring rhythm into the lines.

References to Idital paintings in this novel are a vital element in the storyline for Sannyasi- the prodigal son of the protagonist Antaraa to move out of the village. So, I wanted to have an Idital painting for the cover. I thank artist Raghunath Thakur from Kalahandi for the cover design. I am also thankful to Sri Satya Patnaik and Sri Ashok Parida at Black Eagle Books for their contribution in shaping this gripping storyline into another masterpiece Odia novel for a global audience. I would love to hear your feedback on the novel at: tapanpanda@gmail.com.

Dr Tapan K Panda

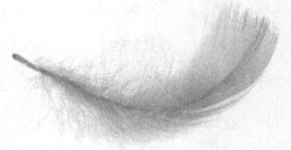

CHAPTER-1

It was the festival of spring. Forest and mountains rejoiced with its arrival in a mosaic of colours. The calm air emerged and brought the fragrance of flowers and touched the heart. From the wintry shades of narrow lanes and alleys emerged gaily clad humanity. Flowering mustard field, pale like melting gold, swept across miles and miles of even land and the sweet scent of the young flowers, the raining petals, and lo! The cooing of cuckoos bustling about on their gaudy black wings, intercepting the flight, and the flowering of the mango tree, a sign of its youthfulness, announced the arrival of spring. As the blooming flowers of the mango tree remoulded to fruit, the brightly coloured, unusual-shaped Mahua flowers opened their petals, and the sweet fragrance swelled in the air. The raining petals of the flowers dropped like melting stars in the free spirit of the night, frenzied man, and beast, and engulfed the surrounding villages in the sense of rapture and enchantment.

Sweet Mahua (*Madhuca or Butter tree*) flowers with an intoxicating fragrance sometimes attracted the bears, and they entered the nearby villages. At times to collect Mahua flowers, the young girls in the village enter the forest, and as soon as they realize that they are in the mid of the forest, they run back home to save their lives from the wild animals. Whenever a herd of elephants enters the village, attracted by the fragrance of Mahua flowers, there is devastation. They destroy houses, trample babies and lift people with their trunks and crush them. They were nothing less than the notorious dacoits who ransack the houses. Still, the fragrance of the flower intoxicated both humans and the beast.

It was summer, and the Tendu (*Asian Ebony*) tree was laden with ripe fruits, and Mahua flowers bloomed. The ripe and delicious, sweet fruits of Tendu dropped from the trees in summer, which was enough to satiate the hunger. By the time the last fruit on the tree was about to fall, the black plum had already started changing its colour, and it seemed as if the wildwood was displaying its wealth one after another. There were not only the mangoes and varieties of berries but also the colourful Palash (*Flame of the Forest or Butea Monosperma*) flowers blooming like fire.

As soon as the tender leaves of Tendu sprout, the tribals get ready to pluck the leaves to sell those to the contractor to earn their living. They sold those for a lesser price to the contractor than the price fixed by the government. The tribals take Tendu leaves from the small merchants to roll and make bidi (*a cheap type of cigarette made from tobacco and wrapped in leaf*) to earn some money. Women in the house weave mats and make brooms out of palm leaves, and men weave mats for the doorway with Khus-Khus (*a mat made out of natural vitriver which is a fragrant grass with a sweet aroma*) and sell them in *Kantabanji* and Nuapada. The wealth of the forest, like Tendu leaves and seeds of the Sal (*shorea robusta*) tree, help the tribals to earn their living. The number of boars and deers in the forest has reduced as they were hunted for festivals and marriage ceremonies. It seems now the forest belongs to the government, and these tribals think that government is a creature, and they don't know how does it look? The forest guard says that he is a government servant, and if they cut wood from the forest, then they will be imprisoned and tortured in jail, and if they collect firewood, they will be penalized. Though they have never seen the government, they have seen the lorries entering the forest at midnight, and the next day they could see empty land which was once overgrown with trees. Still, they couldn't understand the mystery behind it; otherwise, they would have asked the government, whom they had never seen.

There is no more dense forest that existed before surrounding villages, mountains, and streams. There was greenery on the riverside. On the top of a hillock, one could see vultures flying with their wings spread and people following the flight of the birds. From a distance, a vulture sitting on a tree looked like an old man with a hunch. It waited for it's prey or a corpse to pounce on it and tear the flesh apart. It took almost one and half days for the vultures to devour the corpse, and sometimes these corpses were devoured by birds of prey, dogs, and jackals. Despite the rotting smell of the decomposed dead bodies, these tribes cooked their food under the tree, ate, and slept. They were habituated to the norm of life and collected the skin and the skeletons of the animals and loaded those in the bullock cart. The bullock cart owner presented his terms and conditions so that the cart didn't get unsanctified. A rug was spread over the cart, and the skeleton was lifted carefully and kept on it. Though the skeleton looked clean without flesh, still the air was filled with the rotting smell. The cart moved through the village road and finally reached the storehouse of *Rehman* Miyan, which was at *Kisinda*.

Rehman Miyan was very calculative.

He asked- How old is the corpse?

-Why is it wet?

-Did you dip it in water so that the weight would increase?

- I will deduct half of the amount.

- Take it back and bring it after a month.

They were worried. Again, after a month? From where will they arrange the bullock cart? How will they arrange the money for it? How much will they earn after selling the skeleton so that they can pay the bullock cart owner and divide it among themselves?

Rehman acts as if he is going to lock his storehouse and go. They sit down under the shade of the tree and wait. They must go back to the village before sunset and must return the bullock cart to its owner. *Rehman* was ready to go home, but still, they were sitting under the shade of the tree.

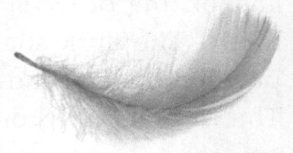

CHAPTER-2

Sanyaasi...Sa... nya... si....., Sa.... nya.... Si!

The forest, mountains, rivers, and the leaves of the trees echoed with the name as if the trees were asking for the leaves, the mountain was asking for the stones, and the river was asking to the stream- *Have you seen Sanyaasi?*

The leaves were fluttering in the wind as if they were conversing with each other, but their language was beyond *Sanyaasi's* mother's comprehension. If she could have comprehended, then she could have known where *Sanyaasi* was. In the meantime, *Sarasi* was in the dense forest, and as the sun was still shining brightly, she wasn't scared. The sound of the beetles, katydids, crickets, and grasshoppers didn't scare her too. It was her long battle with the forest that continued. Sometimes she walks deep into the forest to ask the forest, where is her *Sanyaasi? Sanyaasi* fell in love with the beauty of the forest and never returned.

Sarasi again called out *Sanyaasi... Sanyaasi...* in her trembling voice. Her words resounded in the forest, and in conclusion, there was utter silence. *Sarasi* stood under the Simuli *(Red Silk Cotton or Bombax Cieba)* tree for a while as she was uncertain whether to go further or to return back. She ran a little further and saw the river, which seemed to be squeezed between the ridges, and on the other side of the river was the rest of the forest. The dark shadows of the voluminous trees and puzzled bushes had become the structure of the forest. The trees stood proud and tall as the protectors of the exigent ground, as the impregnated bushes concealed the land beneath from the vibrant portals of the open sky. *Sanyaasi*'s mother could hear the rhythmic tune of the stone cutters working at a distance. Her son was attracted by the rhythmic sound of the stone cutters and went to the quarry but never returned. People narrated many tales; she heard those but couldn't believe them. Sometimes she thinks that the witch has hidden her son within those stones. The witch has stolen her son. *Sarasi* again shouted as she thought maybe her son would hear her voice and run towards her with a smile.

Can this boy understand the feelings of a mother? Who doesn't want that her son should be in front of her? When he was a child, he left with Father Emanuel. At that time, he was only seven years old. There was a festival in the village, and a camp was arranged by *Sahib* in the Christian *Padaa* (ghetto). Many people were getting converted into Christianity, and *Sahib* was blessing each of them. Someone came and asked her: 'Where is your son *Sarasi*?'

Are you taking care of him? *Sarasi* said: He is playing outside, maybe near Jamuna's aunt's house. He must be around.

: You sit and draw and do the household work. Let your son go to the Christian ghetto and turn into a Christian.

: 'What did you say?' Dropping the bunch of earthen straw, *Sarasi* left her work and came out running.

She said: My son is always with me; then how did he travel so far and go to the Christian ghetto? Are you telling the truth, *Dada(Uncle)*?

: Why will I speak lie? I was walking down and saw that *Sahib's* wife had made your son sit next to her at the table.

: *Dada*, if you saw my son, then why didn't you bring him from there?

Sarasi was helpless. Why did *Sahib's* wife make her son sit at the table? They are untouchable. Even *Kandha Sabar* (Another tribal community) don't drink water from them. People avoid them, but Emanuel *Sahib* says that there is nothing called caste and all humans are equal. If you want to become a Christian, then you must forget about caste. You all are the sons of God. The most loving son of God is Jesus. All are equal in front of God. She has heard the speech of Father Emanuel many times. It feels good to hear him, and his arguments seem to be justified, but to be a Christian isn't easily acceptable. *Kisan Khadia* (another tribe) have converted to Christianity, but they still believe in the caste system. They even don't touch them. *Sarasi* was restless. She thought the tribal *Kandha* boys may beat her *Sanyaasi*. She hastily ran towards the Christian ghetto. *Sanyaasi's* father was not around…had gone to Chunakhali. Whom will she speak to…?

: *Dada*, why didn't you pull him back?

: I would have brought him back if he had been willing to come. Your son was drawing something on paper, and resting her head on both the palms, *Sahib's* wife was looking at what he was drawing.

: What is the use of drawing? Let that go to hell. What

did he draw that he was showing to *Sahib*'s wife? I hope you aren't fooling me, *Dada*. Tell me, where did my son go? *Sanyaasi* is precious to me. If his father comes to know, then I will be in trouble. He will kill me. *Sarasi* was crying bitterly.

: Why will I lie to you, *Sarasi*? I swear. I would have brought him back, but as your son is a child, nothing would have happened to him; if the people had come to know that I had entered the Christian ghetto, they would have troubled me.

Sarasi ran like an insane person. If the wife of *Sahib* converts her son into a Christian, then what will happen? His father will not spare her.

Sarasi wasn't in her senses. If she had been in her senses, she would have thought that they weren't allowed in that area. If, by chance, she touches the food grains kept for drying, then the men and women will come forward to beat her. But how can she tolerate her son being converted to Christianity in front of her eyes?

Sarasi stood at a distance and saw that *Sahib*'s wife was sitting on a chair. She was very fair like goat milk and had red lips and golden hair. Though she was wearing a saree, she still didn't look like an Indian. She was smiling and whispering something into her son's ear. Was it a magical hymn. Was it *Dubon*'s chant (magical hymns to control people)? She was scared to enter the camp. From a distance, she could see her son writing something with a pen with a high level of concentration. *Sanyaasi* had never been to school, so he didn't know how to write. Did *Sahib*'s wife hypnotize him? Who knows if one can be hypnotized by reading *Dubon* or not? Otherwise, how can half of the people in the village give up their age-old religion and adopt Christianity?

She felt as if her son had been hypnotized, but she was unable to do anything. She could have snatched her son away from the clutches of a tiger, but she feared *Sahib*'s wife.

Sarasi knew that her husband had a lot of dreams for *Sanyaasi*. He thought that *Sanyaasi* would be educated and become a collector. Though *Sanyaasi* wasn't born at that time still, his father dreamt that his son would become a Collector. He will sit in the Collector's jeep and visit the villages to give justice to people like him. That's why he never addresses *Sanyaasi* by his name; instead, he addresses him as Collector. He often asked: *Sarasi*, do you know the meaning of Collector?

: How will I know?

: Collector means the king of the area. Did you understand *Sarasi*? Your son will become a Collector, and will ride on an elephant.

Sarasi said: You are just dreaming. We don't have enough to eat a square meal, then why are you dreaming? Where is the dream in starved eyes?

: Who doesn't dream? Tell me, *Sarasi*. Don't you dream?

Though *Sarasi* mocked her husband, was she not dreaming about her first child? She thought that it didn't matter if her son didn't become a Collector, but he shouldn't do the work of collecting dead animal bones and skeletons, which they do.

Sanyaasi was born during difficult days. When he was born, there was a lot of disputes among the people. The wife of Ghanshyam *Satnemi* did something foolish, which aggravated the situation. In the afternoon, Sunaa went to the pond belonging to the upper-class people and took bath there even though she knew that Satnemi were prohibited from taking a bath there. Why did she make this mistake knowingly? She may know the reason. *Bata Nayak* saw Sunaa when she was climbing the stone staircase of the pond. Instead of apologizing to *Bata Nayak*, she argued and quarrelled with him and said- When you make merriment with us without anyone's knowledge, -at that time, is there nothing called untouchability? Then tell me, how did the pond get defiled when I took a bath there? She again said egoistically- Let me reveal the truth that though *Bata Nayak* has a wife at home, he still has an eye on me. Let all of them know about this so-called gentleman. For a while, Sunaa forgot about her own dignity and spoke ill about *Bata Nayak*. Everyone came to know about it, and people of the higher community with arms came to their ghetto. Slowly the quarrel spread like wildfire. People attacked each other, and in that process, Sunaa's brother-in-law beat and killed *Bata Nayak*'s son. The people of the higher community, in anger, burnt their houses. Women were wailing, and the police, without knowing the details, arrested the people of their community. *Antaraa* had just arrived from *Kisinda*, he was innocent, but he was beaten by the people. He was badly injured, but the police took him to the police station.

Sunaa wanted to leave the village and go to her father's house in *Kantabanji*. Her mother-in-law was wailing and saying that she had made a mistake by making a girl from the town her daughter-in-law. *Sarasi* was pregnant at that time and was about to deliver. Her house was destroyed and burnt, and there was smoke everywhere. As there was no place to take rest so her mother-in-law made her sit under a *Mahula* tree. People were busy collecting their clothes and utensils from the debris. Some of them were ready to clean their house. *Purandara,* the old man, was shouting- Let it remain that way. The Collector will come and inspect. If you arrange things properly, then what will he inspect? You won't get any money to reconstruct your house.

Her mother-in-law left her and went to arrange the house as she was expected to deliver at any time. Her mother-in-law thought that at any time her daughter in law will deliver, then where will her grandson stay? She ignored what *Purandara* said and was busy with her work. *Sarasi* was sad as *Antaraa* was injured, and the police arrested him. *Purandara* said - The police would send him to the hospital for treatment.

She had an extremely strong cramp that took her breath away and made her unable to talk; the muscles inside were slowly twisting harder and harder until it became almost unbearable, tears rolled down, blinding her, and she felt as if her stomach was trying to squeeze out all its content. *Sarasi* screamed- Where did you go, Mother? Hold me! But there was no one to listen to her. She was sweating profusely and caught hold of the Mahua tree. Darkness surrounded her; she was unable to cover herself and said, 'Dear God, please close your eyes. Don't see this pain of a woman. Tears rolled down, and she felt as if a stream was erupting, ripping the core of the earth. The cry of the new-born rang in the air.

: Aah! The wealth of my life has arrived said her mother-in-law and ran towards her with those muddy hands. She tried to find out the gender of the child and again ran to clean her muddy hand. *Sarasi* was extremely tired, and her mother-in-law picked up the new-born from the ground. Still, the umbilical cord was attached. Her mother-in-law said- push, push. Why are you looking at me? Whom will I call now in the village? She wailed- *Antaraa*, your wife is going to die today. *Sarasi*, how long will you keep the child attached to you? Push with all your strength.

It was an enthralling moment. The new-born was in the hands of his grandmother and was looking at his mother. *Sarasi* wanted to hold the baby and kiss him. She was leaning on the trunk of the *Mahula* tree and was pushing with a lot of strength. She will survive for this innocent child, for her Collector. Finally, the arduous situation subsided. Her mother-in-law covered her with the saree, and the baby's cord was cut. The old lady was happy with her grandson. She forgot for a moment that her son was in the police station.

Sarasi was sad thinking about her husband. She thought- if he had been there, he would have been so happy. He must be in pain as his leg was injured badly. Hope he didn't get a fracture. If he had been in *Kisinda* for one more hour, he would have escaped from this trouble. Police have arrested all the men in their community, and they are charged with murder. No one knows when they will be released or not. Was the child supposed to be born on such a day? She wanted to inform *Antaraa* that he was blessed with a son. He will become happy and will again dream of his son becoming a Collector.

Who can stop anyone from dreaming? The day *Antaraa* was released from jail, he held his son in his arms and said: Your name is Collector. Listen, *Sarasi*, my son will be a Collector. Right from childhood Collector was very soft-hearted and apathetic. He was forcibly sent by his mother to play with the other children. *Sarasi* was always scared, thinking that her son shouldn't become a recluse, so because of his personal traits, she addressed him as *Sanyaasi*, but she never imagined that one-day *Sanyaasi* would go to *Sahib*'s camp. It's true that the boy goes to the forest and sits near the bank of the river for hours together but why to *Sahib*'s camp?

One day *Sanyaasi* was writing something on a piece of paper, and *Sahib*'s wife was watching him very keenly. She couldn't understand how to bring her son back from *Sahib*'s wife. She called out *Sanyaasi.... Sanyaasi*. As if her voice broke the concentration of *Sanyaasi*. He looked around and saw his mother, jumped from the chair, and ran towards his mother.

Sarasi hugged her son and murmured something. *Sanyaasi*'s body was bare, and he was wearing only a pant, but *Sarasi* was dusting something from his back. What was she dusting? Is it the dust or the evil eye of *Sahib*'s wife? Both were going back home, and she saw *Sahib*'s wife waving at them. Whom is she calling? Is she calling her or her son? Why is she calling? What did the boy do? She pretended as if she didn't see and went away from there, but *Sahib*'s wife followed them and called: Listen!

Sarasi turned back, walked a few steps, and asked: Why are you calling? My son will not become a Christian. His father isn't there. He has been to *Durikhal*. Pastor *Padhi* called her: Listen! *Chamaara*[1]'s wife.

---

1   Chamaara - A Member of an Indian caste whose traditional occupation is leatherwork/ bone collection from dead animals

She felt as if she has lost her son. Her eyes were filled with tears, and she said: I am going. His father isn't there. After walking a few steps, she beat her son and said angrily: Why did you go to the camp?

Sanyaasi cried loudly. Pastor *Padhi* smiled and said: Please listen to what *Mem Sahib* is saying. Why are you uttering nonsense?

Sahib's wife brought the paper and showed her. There were pictures of the cow, parrot, and flowers drawn similarly to the pictures drawn by *Sarasi* on the wall of her house. Pastor *Padhi* said: The little boy has learned to draw from you. *Mem Sahib* is very happy. She wants to take your son. Give her your son so that he becomes something in his life.

Sarasi was startled. She thought, is her son, not a human being? Can't he earn his living when he grows up? How can *Mem Sahib* make him something in his life? *Sarasi* was scared. She thought that the lady was a witch, a vampire. If she isn't a vampire, then how can she love her son so much? She will lure her son and then suck his blood. *Sarasi* ran as fast as she could with her son as if she was trying to escape death. Though *Sanyaasi* got beatings by his mother, he tolerated it. After a while, he opened his palm and showed his mother two chocolate.

CHAPTER 3

*A*ntaraa felt a stabbing pain as if a hot, sharp knife was slicing through his skin and into his muscles and bones, as though his leg had frozen, and a bolt of lightning had struck his body from head to toe. He limped and dragged himself in searing pain and fever. Though the distance to his house was less, he was unable to walk. The evening was approaching, and the jackals were making a range of howling and barking calls. At a distance was the village cremation ground, and on the backside if it was their ghetto which was totally disconnected from the rest of the village.

Antaraa felt like taking a rest for some time, but he thought that if he took a rest, then it would be too late. He may feel lazy to get up again, so he should muster his courage and march ahead. He felt as if he was about to die; his throat was parched, his eyes were burning, and his body was severing. *Antaraa* thought that it was the fruit of his karma. He suffers from a fever every month, and it sucks his strength and vigour. He had never experienced it before, but since the day he committed the sin, he has been suffering regularly. Though he never spoke to anyone regarding it, he could understand that it was the fruit of his sin.

The fever lasts for a fortnight. *Sarasi* grinds the herbs, prepares the medicine, and makes him drink, and he always feels nauseated while drinking the bitter medicine.

Sarasi says: Let's go to the other side of the village, where there is a hospital, and consult the doctor. He will give the injection, and you will be fine, but *Antaraa* never agreed to go as he feared the injection. *Sarasi* tried her best to make him understand, but *Antaraa* was always rigid in this regard. Finally, *Sarasi* gave up, cried, and cursed her fate. She said: I gave birth to four children, but I am here alone as if I am a barren woman. All of them left me. I am still alive. You will understand when I die. No one will be there to give you a drop of water, and then you will remember me. I lost my children; why am I alive? Why am I not dying? She cried bitterly.

Sometimes people stand for a while and listen to her cry. *Antaraa* shouts at her and says- Calm down. Don't cry so much. It's in our destiny, and it has happened, isn't it? In this world, who is for whom? Neither you are for me, nor I am for you. Everything is an illusion. Did you understand? The world is an illusion.

A poet has said:

'Who you think as your kith and kin.

After you leave your body, they will call you a ghost.'

Sometimes *Antaraa* recites a few lines for *Sarasi* to make her understand. *Sarasi* stops crying and gets up from there in anger. *Antaraa* gets annoyed with her behaviour and sometimes beats her. He says: You are an awful wife. Do you have money to go to the doctor? Is the doctor your husband that he will give the medicine free of cost?

Antaraa and *Sarasi* lived their life in happiness and sadness. *Antaraa* suffered from intermittent fever every month and recovered but became weaker and weaker.

Antaraa's throat was parched, but instead of going home, he was following the light of a lantern. Today he has earned enough money as he went to *Kisinda* and sold the bones to *Rehman*. He won't beg *Sarasi* to give him some money. She is a stubborn lady, and it doesn't matter if he asks her for money or not, but she gets angry and quarrels. Sometimes she hides the money in the box and sometimes under the utensils. If he finds it, then that's fine; otherwise, he can't do anything. Wives aren't at all trustworthy, and even God won't be able to know their secrets.

Antaraa checked the money pouch, which he tied to his waist. There was a sense of contentment. He dragged himself and reached their ghetto, and instead of going home, he went to *Kalandar Kisan's* liquor shop. It's not only the shop of *Kalandar Kisan*; it's his life. He feels restless if he doesn't go there. The thoughts elated his mood, and his happiness knew no bounds. He thought he had to take a few more steps to wet his parched throat.

He sat outside *Kalandar's* shop and called *Kalandar*. The forest guard was sitting on the wooden bench. *Antaraa* could never tolerate this person.

He was angry and said: Why is this person sitting here? Why don't these guards die?

: *Kalandar*, give me a bidi and the matchstick.

: Are you a *Sahib*? Go from here. I don't have a bidi.

: Are you giving it to me for free? Why are you talking nonsense?

Antaraa took out his money pouch and showed it with a lot of pride.

: Will you pay me the previous balance amount today?

Antaraa didn't say anything. He was charmed when he looked at the money.

Kalandar said: Give the money.'

Antaraa opened his pouch and took out a ten rupee note.

: Take this and give me bidi and liquor.

Antaraa took the bidi from *Kalandar* and smoked. He said: Now give me the liquor bottle.

The forest guard laughed and asked: Did you steal?

: Is there any scarcity of thieves in this village that I will go and steal? The thieves are everywhere in the form of gentlemen. He said this indicating to the forest guard.

The forest guard was sitting quietly, eating fish, and drinking liquor. As he heard *Antaraa*, he looked at him.

He said- How come you have so much guts to speak to me in this way?

: Yes, I am saying that you are a thief. What can you do? Will you beat me? Beat... I will repeat again and again and in front of everyone.

: You scumbag! You beggar. What did you say? The forest guard got up to beat *Antaraa* but lost his control and sat down on the bench again.

This was the time when *Kalandar Kisan* did a brisk business, so he didn't want that any mess should be created over there. It's true that he didn't like the forest guard as he knew that he was a scoundrel. He said to *Antaraa*: Go to your home. Don't try to create any problems here.

Why should I go? I have paid you money for the drink. Is this his father's shop?

The forest guard was trying, again and again, to get up, but he couldn't as he was completely drunk. If he wouldn't have been drunk, then he would have beaten *Antaraa* black and blue. He was dazed and slept on the wooden bench. *Antaraa* said: He is a nasty person, the enemy of the forest. He has exploited the forest and has constructed a house at *Ganjam (an erstwhile district of Odisa)*.

Dhumra was drunk. In the state of intoxication, he said: We should pee on his face.

Kalandar acted as if he was annoyed and said: If you want to spout nonsense, then go from here. I will close the shop.

Why should we go? I want to drink. If you don't have liquor, give mahuli *(Country Liquor)*.

Kalandar had kept separate glasses for the *Chamaars*. He has also kept a few empty Coca-Cola bottles for these *Chamaaras*. He brought a bottle half filled with liquor and kept it on the ground. He said- I am deducting the money that you owe. You lame man!

Antaraa said- Give me some peanuts.

: Do you think you will get peanuts for free?

: You are giving the forest guard so many things to eat, but you aren't giving us anything.

: I am warning you. Don't pester me. You may leave now. Do you think that I am waiting for your money?

Kalandar had an eye on the pocket of the forest guard. *Antaraa* knew that *Kalandar* might scold him, but he will give him some peanuts. It doesn't matter if he charges a little money for that. *Kalandar* brought some peanuts and gave them to *Antaraa*.

He said- Give me two rupees.

By that time, *Antaraa* had already taken a sip. He chewed a few peanuts and again gulped the liquor from the bottle. \

: *Kalandar*, give me one more glass.

Kalandar had a knack for doing business. He has seen the money in *Antaraa's* waist pouch. He will slowly empty *Antaraa's* pocket in such a way that *Antaraa* will never realize.

Kalandar said: Go to your house. Your wife must be waiting for you.

: I am in pain because of the fever *Kalandar*. Please, give me some more to drink. Let me get rid of this torment.

Kalandar was busy attending to the other customers. All of them were drunk and in a different world, and *Kalandar* was making them dance to his tune. In the meanwhile, three more customers came to his shop. He was busy entertaining the new customers. *Antaraa* stood up as he was ready to leave. *Kalandar* immediately brought a glass of *Mahuli* and poured it into *Antaraa's* glass.

By that time, *Kalandar* had already collected twenty rupees from *Antaraa*, but still, he said- Give me another ten rupees as I have given you the peanuts, bidi, liquor, and also *Mahuli*. *Antaraa* didn't say anything and gave him another five rupees.

Antaraa gulped *Mahuli* and said- *Daaktar*, where are you?

Dhumra, who was also drunk, said- *Antaraa*, are you dreaming?

: No, *Dada*. I am remembering *Daaktar*. Where did that young boy vanish? It is the conspiracy of Ganjam's *Gantai Sahu* and the forest guard. They have taken away all the young boys of the village as bonded laborers. Can you find any younger boys in the village? Among my three sons, *Daaktar* was the second one.

Dhumura was half asleep and a bit boozed. He woke up from his sleep and said: You are right.

Antaraa's heart was filled with sadness. He thought, maybe somewhere in a different place, his son must be leading a miserable life. What would he be eating? Is he married or not?

The second one was eighteen years old, but he wasn't slothful like Collector. He was swift and agile. He was working as a labourer for spreading the telephone lines. He was wise, so he didn't prefer to take up the profession of his father. He never listened to anyone. *Antaraa* thought that the elder one would become a collector, but he eloped with a girl. His act was so shameful that *Antaraa* couldn't face the villagers. By that time, his glass was empty. He asked *Kaladar*- Will you give me some more? *Kalandar* tried to ignore him. *Antaraa* gave him a coin and said- Will you give it?

Kalandar laughed and said- Today, this man is partying. He said: Do you know anything about *Shastra (Religious Text)*?

Antaraa said: You will spend your life only by selling liquor. Listen! What does Shastra mean? He recited a few lines:

"So many of your friends have left this mortal world,

Who have taken their wealth and how many?

Never you utter the master Govind's name,

Being selfish you have only made money."

: That's enough. You are a very learned person. Now give me the rest of the amount, and after that, speak about the Shastra and scriptures.

Antaraa had forgotten that *Kalandar* had to return him five rupees. He doesn't know how to calculate, and other than that, in that drunken state, how can he do the calculation? He was also not sound physically and mentally. In a loud voice, he recited a few lines from *Bhaagabat*:

"Man doesn't know about good and bad.

Realizes it at the time of death."

Kalandar was busy extracting money from the drunkards over there. It was only the forest guard who never gave a single penny for his drinks. He walks into *Kalandar*'s shop, behaves affectedly, eats fried fish and chicken, and drinks to the full. But *Kalandar* waits patiently till the time the forest guard is completely drunk and takes away the money from his pocket quietly. The ill-gotten money goes in a shady way. While closing the shop, he lifts the forest guard and makes him lie down on the veranda and purposely throws five or ten rupees on the ground so that after the forest guard gets back to his senses, he will find the money fallen on the ground and won't suspect *Kalandar*.

But that day, the lines recited by *Antaraa* touched his heart. He thought the *Chamaar* knew his secrets. Though the man isn't literate, he has the knowledge of Sastra.

Anyways his son stayed with Emanuel *Sahib*, studied, and visited different places. Maybe from the son, the father gained some knowledge. Though the son became educated, he neither helped his parents nor took care of them. He eloped with the daughter of *Baija Sara* and settled down somewhere in Raipur or Bhopal, and since then, there has been no news about him. Sometimes *Kalandar* feels pity for *Antaraa*. After his son eloped with *Baija Sara's* daughter, there was unrest between the two communities. *Antaraa* was scared; he locked his house and left the place with his family early in the morning. Some of them said that he was hiding in the forest, and some of them said that he was there with his brother-in-law in *Kantabanji*. For the misdeed of the son, the father suffered.

A few of them also said that they had seen *Antaraa* in *Rehman*s storehouse cleaning, drying, and polishing the animal hide. Someone said that he had seen *Antaraa* in Bhopal wearing a new dhoti and kurta and loitering in the marketplace along with his son. But how long can someone stay away from his own place? One day in the evening, the family came back to the village, and the fire, which got extinguished, again aggravated. People who sympathized with *Antaraa* now again started talking about caste. In the meantime, *Baija Sara* had again become a part of his caste by giving a good treat and drinks to his community people but what about *Antaraa*? Will he think about feeding his family of four *Members* or thinking about giving a treat to his community people?

Early in the morning, there was a meeting in their ghetto, and finally, *Antaraa* agreed to give fifteen kgs of rice and two kgs of pulses. *Sarasi* pledged the gold waistband with *Saha*, which she brought from her father's house when she got married to meet the expenses. *Sarasi* shouted and said: You are all envious of my family.

Sarasi had kept the gold waistband for her daughter's marriage, and she knew that it won't be possible for her to repay and get back the pledged gold. Let the sorrow and joy go to hell; they have to survive. But could they survive like humans? People spoke many things about her, and to how many will she answer to keep their mouths shut?

: You have left the village, then why did you come back again? Did your son throw you out of the house?

: Was *Rehman* not able to give you two square meals?

: Four of you left the village, then why did only three of you return? Did you kill one of them?

: Why did you come back to the village? You could have stayed with your brother-in-law, worked in the city, and would have earned a living.

What was left for him there in this place? He has a two-room mud house with a thatched roof which he was not able to repair even after four years. He didn't have any property and a village, for the name's sake. After leaving *Rehman*'s house, he felt as if he was like a weathered leave of a tree. He didn't have any answer to anyone's question. People also gossiped about *Sarasi*, saying that *Sarasi* went to *Rehman*'s storehouse without anyone's knowledge leaving behind her three children. *Antaraa* doesn't know about it, and she returns from *Rehman'* s storehouse with money, and with that money, they feed the people of their community. Some of them said that it was not true as *Rehman* is very stingy, so he can never give her money. Some of them said that *Sarasi* didn't go to *Rehman*; rather, she went to *Bhutapada*, where the Musheerabad Muslims put their tents, and *Parmanand* saw her there.

Antaraa heard the gossip and sat silently for a few days. He was annoyed with *Sarasi* and didn't eat food properly, and after a few days, he left his family and the village.

The second son *Daaktar* was liked the most by *Antaraa*. He was a very capable boy. After *Antaraa* left the house, he took responsibility for the house. He worked as a daily labourer and earned money to feed his family. *Sarasi* thought if *Antaraa* had been there, he would have realized that his son was responsible enough to take care of the family. But as *Antaraa* is a man so he could leave the house to escape the humiliation, but that wasn't possible in the case of *Sarasi*. Then after *Sarasi* never went to *Rehman*'s storehouse even though sometimes her son didn't get any work to do.

People said that *Antaraa* had died. If he had been alive, he would have come to meet his family, but he returned after a year and a half. *Antaraa*'s second son was a very good child. Whatever he earned, he gave a part of it to his mother. With the money he had, he purchased all the necessary things that he needed. He wasn't a regular drinker and sometimes drank along with his friends.

Everything was going on well. *Antaraa* could see his young days in *Daaktar*. Though he got a bad name for his elder son, he thought the second son would make him proud. He had only one sorrow his children didn't know how to skin the animals. They didn't know the other techniques of cutting and polishing the skin. *Haridas gossain* (brahmin priest) had said that everyone had been assigned some work so that they could earn their living. If everyone will do the same job, then who will do the rest? Each work is respectable. The food tastes delicious when eaten, and finally, the same food is excreted.

: Are you sleeping, *Antaraa*? Get out from here. I must close the shop as my lantern has no more kerosene.

Antaraa was dozing. He said- I am going. But he couldn't stand.

: Go quickly. Do you think that I will sit here and look after you?

Antaraa got up from his place with a lot of difficulties. Where will he go? To *Lephrikhol*? To *Sinapali*? *Kantabanji, Bhopal, Andhra, or Raipur*? Where will he go? *Dharamgad*?

He was feeling lighter. He was trying to put his feet on the ground. He remembered people saying that he must have jumped from the peak of the mountain and many more tales. He ignored all those tales and returned as a changed person. He was almost transformed into a saint with wooden beads around his neck - preaching and singing hymns. No one would say that he is *Chamaar Satnemi*.

Sarasi will be surprised to see him. She will ask- where did you go? What were you doing? Where were you all these days that you didn't remember your family? You didn't think about us. Though he imagined what *Sarasi* would say, she didn't ask her anything. She said- I am a woman; where would I have been in search of you? You couldn't tolerate what people said and left us. You didn't think after you left how people would have abused me. They said that I am kept of *Rehman* and that's why you left me. Look! Look! At the boy. See how the boy has taken responsibility for the family. Look at the condition of the boy as he is toiling so hard.

Till then, the father and the son didn't speak to each other. There was no complaint, no anger, and no resentment, but still, they couldn't look into each other's eyes.

The responsibility had made his son look mature, and the father seemed to be immature after giving up all his responsibilities. *Antaraa* looked at the strong arms of his son and felt as if he had grown old. He could understand that after him, his children aren't going to take up his profession. There is no regret for that, but isn't it good to not know the work of a *Chamaar* being a *Chamaar*?

Daaktar didn't show any resentment toward his father. He was busy with his own work. He was very happy as he felt now, he had wings to fly in the open sky. He could see the dead carcasses from the sky and wished to plunge into them. Will he plunge? With this thought, he descends from the sky. Suddenly *Antaraa* was startled at the sight of a half-dead cow. A lovable, beautiful creature suddenly lost its charm and looked so horrible, so frightening as it lay there, legs spreadeagled, a fixed stare in its eyes, and a crow sitting on its back. *Antaraa* made the crow fly away. It flew to a distance and then landed on the ground and sat. He wanted to touch the cow, but he couldn't. He dragged his listless body. There was darkness everywhere. Neither could he see the cow nor himself.

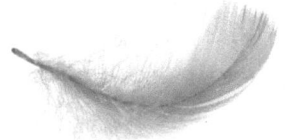

CHAPTER 4

*C*haiti has never seen an ocean. She has heard that it's an endless source of water.

Wherever you see, there is water, water, water everywhere, and the towering waves glide toward the shore and break like thunder on the shore. Animals such as seahorses, clownfish, and sea turtles live on coral reefs. She has seen the sea in the cinema. It's very vast and widespread, and that floats the ship. *Sanyaasi* has been to an island that is very far away. Maybe one can reach it after crossing such vast oceans. *Chaiti* couldn't imagine how will be the country Japan in the mid of the ocean. In the beginning, he took photographs of different places, of the long flyovers and the smooth black roads on which the vehicles plied. The girls looked beautiful, like dolls. After looking at the photographs of the mountains, valleys, streams, and skyscrapers, *Chaiti* thought what a beautiful place *Sanyaasi* had been. But the country which has such beautiful places and people, why did they call *Sanyaasi* there?

Before *Sanyaasi* left, *Chaiti* told him- Look! I am too scared as you will cross so many oceans and go. *Sanyaasi* said: Are you mad? I won't travel by ship. I will travel by airplane, which flies high up in the air like a vulture.

Chaiti was scared. It doesn't matter if it is through water or air, but both are dangerous. It's different if traveling by bus as many people leave the village and come to *Raipur* by bus. The day *Chaiti* boarded the train for *Bhopal*, she was nervous as the train was a big vehicle, and many people from different places were traveling in it. Few of them were getting down, and few of them were boarding the train. The train was also moving at a slow pace stopping every now and then, but still, their destination was too far. What will happen if they miss the station where they must get down? But the train runs on the rails on the ground so there won't be any problem.

Sanyaasi laughed, listening to it. He said: You fool! Can a train go to such a distant place? Don't you know that to go to the country I have to cross two vast oceans and it lies in the mid of the third ocean. Will they construct roads or spread the railway lines on the ocean for you?

Sanyaasi had taught *Chaiti* a little to read and write at home. At least with that little education, *Chaiti* could write her name and read a letter, but she wasn't very much interested in studies, so she could neither read a book nor her knowledge and outlook were good.

Sanyaasi was eager to go, but still, there were apprehensions in his mind; as the time of his departure was nearing, he was becoming more and more restless. He was engrossed in deep thoughts. He didn't have proper food or sleep. *Chaiti* said- If you aren't happy, then please don't go. Is there anyone who is forcing you to go?

: It's not about someone forcing me to go *Chaiti*. It's something else that you won't understand.

: What is that which I can't understand? You have become weak in these few days. Do you think that I can't understand?

Sanyaasi thought that *Chaiti* was a little bit unhappy and that maybe after some time, she will start crying. She will remember the village and think about it. She can't cope with city life and is feeling lonely. He said: It's for Emanuel *Sahib*. I couldn't refuse him.

: What do you want to say? Speak clearly. *Chaiti* said. You don't like this place now, and I, too, don't like it. Let's go back to our village, and if not to our village, then let's go and stay in *Sundarkhol* village or in *Senapalli*.

: I don't have any problem here, *Chaiti*. The matter isn't that. It's a different matter. Tell me do we have any problem here? I am teaching drawing to the children in the Mission and earning, so we can have our food properly. What will we eat if we go to the village? It will be difficult for us to earn a living, and do you think that the village people will welcome us? Won't they harass and disgrace us? I can't go to the village anymore. Tell me did anyone ask you about your caste and clan here? No one is bothered here about what you eat and what you do.

Do you know what the exact matter is? Emanuel *Sahib* is like God to me, and maybe *Mem Sahib* was my mother at my previous birth. What was I able to draw at the age of five years? I used to draw on the rock of the mountain with a piece of chalk. I always drew a tiger pouncing on a deer and the tiger being aimed with an arrow by *Bana* - the hunter. Do you know *Chaiti*, my mother always narrated the tales of *Bana*- the hunter when I didn't get sleep when I was hungry or when I remembered my father. At that time, I visualized the picture in my mind and drew.

I don't know whether the deer looked like a deer and the tiger looked like a tiger or not, but *Mem Sahib* saw it. She called me and made me sit in her car. I was very scared, but she gave me two chocolates. The camp in the Christian ghetto changed my fate. *Mem Sahib* made me draw many pictures, and if my mother wouldn't reach that place, then I would have got many more chocolates.

Sanyaasi suddenly became silent as if he was now in his childhood days. Though he is trying to move forward step by step still can't reach the present.

Chaiti kept her fingers on the hair of *Sanyaasi* and said- You have been telling me the same thing time and again. I don't have any more patience to listen to the same thing again and again about your Godmother. *Chaiti* addresses Emanuel *Sahib*'s wife as *Sanyaasi*'s Godmother.

As if *Sanyaasi* suddenly came back to his senses and said- Is it so painful for you to listen to it again and again? Do you understand? Only two chocolates made me so greedy that I agreed to leave the village. The day Emanuel *Sahib*'s wife told my mother,' Give me your son, I will make him a good human being that day for the whole night, my father sat in the doorway. Not even for once, he dozed as if *Mem Sahib* would enter the house and snatch me away from the family and convert me into a Christian. He thought, how can *Mem Sahib* make me a good human being as she hasn't given birth to me? My father thought: As I don't have any physical disabilities so I will grow up and become a young man, will work, and earn my living, so what good human will she make me?

In the morning, my father said: Let him go. There isn't enough food in the house to feed him properly. If he stays in the Mission, he will get proper food to eat and survive.

As it is said: Even if the elephant stays in the jungle, it still belongs to the king. Let my son go. He will at least get a square meal to eat.

My mother also imagined a plate of hot steaming rice. She was subdued. She said- I will let him go, but my son shouldn't become a Christian.

: Ok, I will tell that to *Mem Sahib*. You don't become sad.

Still, my mother didn't want to leave me. I was thinking, what is my mother's problem if I go? *MemSahib* won't beat me. She makes me sit next to her to draw the pictures and give me the chocolate. Why is the mother so sad when it is discussed leaving me with *Mem Sahib*?

One day *Mem Sahib* came to take me. Her big car came and stopped in front of our house. My mother combed my hair and wiped my face. She gave me a jute bag and said- Listen to what *Mem Sahib* says, and when you think about us, tell *Mem Sahib*. She will bring you here to meet us.

When I remember, the house means? My eyes were filled with tears, and I felt like crying. I suddenly cried, hugged my mother, and said- I won't go anywhere leaving you, Mother. My father tried to make me understand and said- Son, please go. If you go with them, then you will become a Collector. You will visit many places.

: How can I see my mother if I go?

: I will take your mother to meet you. My father forcibly pulled me from my mother's arms and made me sit in *Mem Sahib*'s car. You won't believe *Chaiti*- Look at this hand of mine. My father pulled this hand and dragged me. I can still feel the pain in this hand.

Chaiti was sobbing.

"What happened? Why are you crying, *Chaiti*?"

He kept his hand on *Chaiti*'s hair and said- I always remembered my mother, but my father never came to meet me though he said that he would come along with my mother to meet me.

Sanyaasi came to the village for four days from *Jagdalpur* Mission School. From childhood, he stayed away from the village and the house, so everything seemed to be unknown to him. He couldn't speak with anyone to his heart's content, but when he was in the boarding school, he always remembered his house and his family members. There was a lot of difference between the present and past life. It's like sculpturing pre-historic stone in contemporary design. They have the same features and the same smell of the soil, but someone has sculptured it exquisitely, which makes them different from others.

Sanyaasi always liked the forest. Right from his childhood, he drew many pictures on the smooth grey rock of the mountain. *Sanyaasi* had no friends and, in his sombreness, went to the forest. The forest was very close to him. Though the trees, the river, the stream, and the stones of the mountain are voiceless when they see *Sanyaasi*, it seems they start speaking. *Sanyaasi* took out the flute from his pocket, sat on a rock under the tree, and started playing the chord, the cord of loneliness and pain. The chord mirrored an empty house, an empty vessel, the despair of a hungry child.

He wasn't aware of the girl wearing a red frock with a flower in her hair standing under the *Mahula* tree and listening to the melody of his flute. When *Sanyaasi* realized her presence, she laughed and vanished from sight in the undergrowth.

He kept the flute in his pocket and searched for the girl. By that time, the girl was in the mid of the *Udanti* River and was jumping over the stones swiftly. What is this girl doing in the jungle? Is she not scared? Who is she? He felt as if a fairy is going away from his reach.

: Stop there. Where are you going? Where are you going?

On the other side of the *Udanti* River was a group of rock cutters, and the girl disappeared among the men and women there. Still, *Sanyaasi* moved ahead in search of the red-frock girl. He saw that the girl was cutting the stones with her soft hands. Who can believe that this girl just before sometime left her work as she was attracted by the melody of the flute and came to the other side of the river? There was no expression on her face, and she was cutting the stone quietly as if she didn't know the flute player.

Sanyaasi came back, but the thoughts of the girl kindled his heart. He visited the next day, and it continued as he couldn't stop himself from going to the forest. His heart throbbed, and everything seemed to be sweet and pleasant. The young girl forgot the pain of cutting the stones, was in deep thought, and opened the doors of her heart.

Was it a mistake on his part to be so sentimental regarding *Chaiti* at that time? If all the pains can be forgotten in love, then what is the harm in being so sentimental? What is the problem in living in the dream for a day or for a moment?

He was sad as he had to leave *Chaiti* and go to a faraway place. With whom, under whose supervision will he leave *Chaiti* now? But *Sanyaasi* didn't reveal his feelings and said- We will go back to the village after I come back from the foreign country. We will go together, stay at your father's house, and bring my parents here. Then we will construct our own house and draw the paintings on its walls.

Chaiti was in deep thought away from the cement and concrete house and Bhopal city. There were no vehicles, no illusion of city life, and the strict regimentation of the missionary. As if she is free and on a silent island under the open sky. Her words echoed in the silence and the soft green grass touching her feet. *Chaiti* was half sleepy with her face on *Sanyaasi*'s chest. She could feel the river flowing down the mountain at a distance, a small house with a courtyard, birds flying in the sky, the sound of the flute, the rhythm of the dance, the sound of the birds, and the blue sky.

CHAPTER 5

She arranged the pleats of the saree over her chest. Though her curves weren't seen below the blouse, the mockery of the man hurt her deeply.

: You whore! You have opened a market- Instead of a thrill, a pain ran down her bones. She mustered her courage, engulfed the deep piercing pain, and correctly arranged her saree. It seemed the man could purchase the entire flower garden. Sometimes he pinched the cheeks of someone or spanked the other. They all tried to hide from him like helpless, panicked deer.

The person's name was *Guda*, and the ghetto was under his control. He was the person who gave the shacks on rent in that ghetto. If the huts were made of tin sheets, he charged thousand rupees; if they were thatched houses, he collected seven hundred rupees; and if they were mud houses with plastic-covered roofs, he collected five hundred from the tenants. *Guda* came once a month to collect the rent. It was challenging to arrange five hundred rupees after all the monthly expenditures. So, paying thousand rupees and staying in a better shack was a dream.

Parabaa and *Jhumuri* selected a shack with a tin sheet wall and thatched roof for seven hundred rupees. But as per their business, they needed help to share the same house.

If one is with a customer, the other must stand outside. They didn't have enough money to take two separate shacks, so they agreed to this condition.

Jhumuri had often tried to convince *Parabaa* to leave the place and go to Raipur without anyone's knowledge. Raipur is a prominent place. There are many people and houses, so can't they work as servants in someone's house and earn thousand rupees?

Jhumuri said- Let us go and stay with dignity and if we don't go, how long will we stay here in this hell and tolerate humiliation?

But they could never go. Their destiny had landed them over there. The outside world isn't for them. If they go outside, then someone or the other will recognize them and, here in the flesh, trade what they are doing in exchange for money. They must do that for free as men in the outside world wait like vultures to rip and tear apart their flesh. People will detest them. They have little respect in the ghetto, but they won't get a place to stay there. Sometimes *Parabaa* distastes herself; she cries remembering her family and village.

Whenever *Guda* comes to the ghetto, he goes around and dictates. As he was expected to collect the rent, *Jhumuri* was in the house and counting money. She took out the dirty notes from here and there and spread them on the bed. She called *Parabaa* and said: Come inside. Why are you standing there for an hour?

Parabaa heard *Jhumuri*'s voice and thought will it be possible to arrange five hundred rupees? She knows that *Jhumuri* is very clever, so she can handle things efficiently. Sometimes she holds her like a mother and a friend.

She says: *Parabaa*, who is there for us here? Neither do we have our parents nor a husband. Every day we come across five to twenty-five customers, so we try to win their hearts by speaking pleasingly in a convincing way so that they will think, without them, your life is useless. Give them your best as if they deserve the best. *Parabaa* sometimes feels that there was hunger before so as now. So, desire is like her second wife.

Jhumuri shouted: You slut! With which husband are you sitting? Now *Guda* will come and throw away our belongings.

Parabaa's body shivered when she suddenly remembered him. If *Guda* had loved the skin and the body, there wouldn't have been any issues. All the women in the slum would have come to him. But *Guda* says: I spit on the face of women like you. Thots! With nasty inside and foxy outside. Your bodies are infected. I have nothing to do with your whoredom; I am only concerned about my money. Whether you die or live, I have nothing to do with that. If you sluts are unable to pay the rent, then leave my house. I will make this place a better place to live for other people. It's a waste to give you whores the shacks on rent as you can't pay; I am defamed, and other than that, I must bribe the police. Still, these women always wait for a chance to lure a bad-tempered man like *Guda*. Some of them apply lipstick and give him a sweet smile; some lift their saree to the knee to show their thighs to lure him. *Guda* shouts... I will provide you with a blow, you bimbo!

Every month *Guda* warns that he will throw them out of the ghetto and make it a place for the good people to stay, but it never happens.

Jhumuri left the counting of the notes and came outside and said: Are you deaf? I have been calling you for a long time. Are you not able to hear?

Parabaa speaks significantly less. She asked: Did *Guda* misbehave with you? She didn't give a reply to *Jhumuri*, but *Jhumuri* could read her eyes well. *Parabaa*'s eyes were filled with tears.

: Yes, since then, I am getting lots of pai in my chest.

: Why did you stand there? Why didn't you come from there? Scoundrel! Let him go to hell. Come, come inside the house. We will first throw these seven hundred rupees on his face, and after he goes, I will apply warm mustard oil on your chest so that you feel better.

Jhumuri counted the notes and wrapped them on a piece of paper. *Parabaa* was cleaning the coal stove when *Jhumuri* shouted: Why are you lighting the furnace? For whom are you going to cook? Listen! *Parabaa*! After *Guda* goes, you can go to *Urvashi*'s house and fry dry fish and bring. We will have it with water and rice.

Sometimes *Parabaa* thinks maybe *Jhumuri* was connected to her in her previous birth; otherwise, why does she take so much care of her? She needs to learn how to speak in a polished way and how to do the work. The day she stepped into this hell, someone brought her to *Jhumuri*, gave her the responsibility to look after her, and said: This girl belongs to your caste.

Jhumuri was very much annoyed with the person. She said: Am I doing business here, or have I opened an ashram that you are leaving her here? If I cannot earn a living, why should I take responsibility for someone else? Take her back along with you.

That day for the first time, *Parabaa* heard *Guda's* name. The man said: *Guda* has told me to keep her with you for a few days. Keep these ten rupees with you for the expenditure. When she starts earning, won't that money be yours?

: Ten rupees is needed. You must give me money to feed her for a month. One more thing, if I keep her in my house, then how will I do my business? The man didn't pay any heed to *Jhumuri*. He gave her four hundred rupees and went away from there. *Parabaa* and *Jhumuri* looked at each other for a while, but *Jhumuri* wasn't happy to see *Parabaa*. *Jhumuri* was busy doing her daily chores and was murmuring something in anger. Still, while drinking tea, she offered *Parabaa* a cup of tea. She asked her- Where is your village?

: *Biju Guda*

: Where is that?

: *Sinapali*

: Where is that?

: I don't know.

After *Guda* left, *Parabaa* washed a handful of dried fish in a ladle, sprinkled it with a few drops of mustard oil and went to *Urvashi's* house.: Did you come from Sambalpur? I am from *Aska, Ganjam*. Refrain from telling anyone here that you belong to the *Chamaara* community. The women here are icky, so tell them you belong to the Gowda community. Since then, *Parabaa* has always listened to what *Jhumuri* said.

Urvashi was cutting potatoes as her son wanted to have the fried potatoes along with water rice. *Parabaa* asked: Sister! Is the coal stove still lightened? I want to fry the dry fish.

: Just now, I have ignited the stove as my son wants to eat potato fry and water rice. He is the son of a lawyer, so he throws tantrums. *Urvashi* addresses her son as the lawyer's son because before coming to the ghetto, she was pregnant as she had a relationship with a lawyer. The story of commitment and deceit was again repeated. *Urvashi* says that it was a mistake on her part. She committed a sin, and now she is bearing its fruits. As a servant, she took advantage of the non-availability of the lawyer's wife in the house and was trying to snatch the rights of a married woman, so if not, then who would suffer for the sin? But as she was carrying the child in her womb so she couldn't die. She had a widow aunt who didn't allow her to stay in the house, so she came to the ghetto and gave birth to the baby. The boy asks for good food, so what can she do? She tries her best to fulfil all his demands.

Jhumuri didn't like what *Urvashi* said. She said: If the boy belongs to the lawyer's family, why don't you leave him there? Why are you keeping him in this dirty ghetto?

Urvashi's son goes to a school near the station where the wives of the high-profile people teach the poor children. That's why she cooks early in the morning.

Parabaa kept the ladle on the stove to fry dry fish.

Urvashi asked: Where did the demon go?

: Yes, sister! Look! How tightly he gave a blow on my chest. I have pain.

She laughed and said: Why did you show your chest to that devil?

: Why should I offer? I covered myself properly in front of him.

: Let that devil die. You are a simple and sober girl, so he misbehaved with you. He won't dare to touch my body.

Parabaa knew very well that to stay there or not stay there depended on *Guda*. *Urvashi* may speak many things behind him, but she can't utter a word in front of him. The dry fish was almost fried, and the smell of it made her hungry. Sometimes when she gets proper food to eat, she remembers her parents. What will they be eating? How are they surviving?

Her father always sat and ate along with her. He used to feed her the first nibble and then eat. He used to say: After three sons, I have a daughter. I will get you married either in *Kantabanji* or in *Titilagarh*. Your brothers will embellish you with ornaments.

: Father! I won't go anywhere.

: If you don't get married, what will the people say? They will say: Four men are in the house, but they couldn't find a groom for the girl? He then says to his second son: *Daaktar*, You will give a necklace to my daughter.

: What is that necklace?

: It's a gold necklace, and the jeweller makes it.

All her brothers became selfish and went away. Her father suffered from intermittent fever, and because of the problem with his leg, he couldn't go and work. But does hunger understand poverty? It's a poor person who knows the pain of hunger.

Her mother was working in *Kisinda* in *Rehman's* storehouse. Throughout the day, her father used to sit on the veranda and grunt. People in the village gossiped about her mother, and a few old people mocked her. *Parabaa* was annoyed by all these. In anger, she said: Father, you are old, so you can't work, then why are you grunting? Can't you understand that?

: Your mother is a characterless woman. She is the mistress of *Rehman*.

: Father, if you speak such nasty things, I will leave the house.

: Will you run away? Go, am I restricting anyone? All your brothers left, so what more will you do for me?

These words of Father hurt *Parabaa* deeply. She thought that she was the life of her father, and without her, her father couldn't stay. How can her father speak like this? But later, she could understand the pain of her father.

With so much anger and pain in his heart, her father recited two lines:

"You had made your mind like rock,

Once you die, nobody is yours".

Parabaa's eyes were filled with tears. *Urvashi* said: Are you going to burn the dish? What are you thinking? The dry fish smells burnt. *Parabaa* became conscious. She took the ladle and came back to her shack.

Parabaa was worried about her mother. She worked hard to feed the family, but her father was always cynical. If he doesn't have the strength to work, why does he always make so much of hue and cry?

Naresh gave him his drum to repair once, but he couldn't tie the skin to it and requested others to help him. With a lot of difficulties, he tied the skin to the drum loosely, and when Naresh came and beat the drum, it sagged, and he scolded him. *Naresh* said- If you cannot do it, then why didn't you accept the work? Why did you spoil the piece of skin? How much have I spent on this? You can't see correctly, you don't have strength, and you said you would repair the drum. I won't give you a single penny.

Once upon a time, her father was well-known for making drums. He tied the skin tightly to the drum, and it resonated very well. Still, now he couldn't do it, so *Naresh* insulted him, and that day, it was evident that his father couldn't work anymore.

Father can't be blamed for everything. Instead, her brothers should be accused. The elder one became a Christian to marry the daughter of *Baiju Sara*. The second one left the house for work and didn't come back. And the youngest one was short-tempered, lazy, and good-for-nothing. He loved *Kundaa* but left her. He was motivated by his friends, and he joined the Naxals.

Kundaa's mother was a widow, but they had a billy goat, which was the source of their earnings. The billy goat was tall and robust. It was the best of all the billy goats in the village and was regarded as the incarnation of God. The villagers brought them so that she could conceive. When people come to leave their doe, they come with the vermilion and leaves to feed the billy goat. They worshipped it as God and left their doe with *Kundaa*'s mother.

Kundaa's mother said: Go now. When God is happy, your doe will conceive.

To make the doe conceive was a pious ceremony. There was no unpleasantness. *Parabaa* had seen the copulation many times. It was seraphic.

Parabaa met *Kundaa* in the same ghetto. *Jhumuri* informed her that a girl from her village, *Bijapali*, had come, and she knew her.

Parabaa was dumbstruck when she heard this. She asked: Are you telling the truth, *Jhumuri*? Who is that unfortunate one? *Parabaa* couldn't control her anxiousness and ran towards the shack located on the other side of the ghetto. *Kundaa* was sitting on the veranda. She couldn't believe her eyes when she saw *Kundaa*. She said- You would be my sister-in-law, then why did you come to this hell?

Kundaa cried bitterly. *Parabaa* also wept and said *Kundaa*- Please, don't cry. Can you tell me if you don't say? You had everything then. What was the necessity to come here? How is your billy goat?

: It died, that's why we are in this condition. It became mad and didn't listen to anyone. It attacked people, and once it went to *Kisinda*. People said it died on the railway line and my mother searched for it but couldn't find it.

: Did you go to my brother's camp in the forest? *Parabaa* asked. *Kundaa* was silent.

: Tell me the truth. You are talking about the billy goat but not saying anything about your life. What about that forest guard?

Kundaa didn't have words to speak. Listening to the name of the forest guard from *Parabaa*, she again started crying. *Parabaa* said- Don't cry. It was in our fate. What can we do? Please don't tell anyone that I am here. I will also keep the information private. If you feel hungry, please come to me. She will take care of *Kundaa*. *Parabaa* also started crying. She was now playing the character of *Jhumuri*. *Parabaa* hugged *Kundaa*.

CHAPTER 6

Waiting all along, this year the rain also didn't come. The whole of the forest was getting burnt in the hot sun. The creeper and bushes, which had encircled like citizens earlier, dried up slowly and appeared like a barren civilization.

Udanti River dried up, losing its beauty like a middle-aged woman. The trees like teak, rosewood, *sal* (Shorea Robusta), Piasal (*Sacred Fig*), Terminalia *Arjuna*, and *Gambhiraa (Gimelina Arborea)*, which had been standing tall for ages, like land owners, laid bare and looked helpless. The despair breathing from the mountains and hills was flaring u the whole earth. The earth became dry and developed cracks. From a distance, one could hear the sound made by the stone cutters, devoid of their melodious songs.

In between, Mango and Jamun *(Black Plum)* trees bore fruits and were standing inundated. Neither the elephants were seen, nor even the langurs *(monkeys)* were jumping from one to the other branch.

The thunder of the rain could be heard at a distant village- in *Nabrangpur* or *Nuagao*n. Sometimes lightning could be seen in the far northern or southern sky. Sometimes the sky was covered with clouds for the whole of the afternoon. Looking at the clouds, people with higher hopes came out of their houses smiling and said- See! It's going to rain. The clouds had arrived like mothers of seven children. The most hopeful ones would come to the village roads, lighting a bidi, raising the garden fences, or murmuring a few lines from an old song. Some of them got drunk to the nose and were swinging like drunken elephants. They started to rejoice at the sight of the clouds expecting rain.

The sky was covered with a dark blanket, and darkness enveloped the entire place. It was as if the hanging banket would engulf the whole forest. Joining the waists and clubbing hands, the trees wanted to dance on the merry-go-round. But alas! They were so far away from each other that even if they extended their hands, they could not touch each other's waist- what horrible days are these! The clouds were dropping down, but they were losing their rhythm. With the arrival of the shadows, it seemed as if the trees started rejoicing, but slowly, the clouds subsided, and their rejoicing turned into an ordeal.

Clouds were waning, and the helpless human couldn't hold them. The trees were standing tall waspishly, and birds had already left their nest, and few of them alive were crying as if pleading the clouds not to go. Who knows- being sad and hurt by the behaviors of the non-romantic forests, the clouds had found their way out. The clouds distanced themselves; the helpless human beings couldn't stretch their hands to hold them. The trees were standing dumbfounded. The birds were lost a long time back. A few who could survive due to good luck were calling the clouds elegiacally -in their languages: stay on please stay on.

The clouds have taken a vow that they won't stay. It was their travel path, so they stopped there for a while;

otherwise, what goodwill do they have along with this village?

Even if you stretch your hands, you cannot touch the clouds. Even a man's chest wind doesn't touch his body. Showing its enchanting youth, sometimes the clouds ran away to other villages. The humans with parched throats are left with emptiness and despondency. They had prepared the land for cultivation from days of burning the forest. They would have offered country liquor and chicken blood to mother earth. But the Lord of rain never shows his benevolence.

Lord Indra is angry. He must be appeased. People consult the priest (Dishari Jaani). You must pamper Lord Indra- by drenching salad juice and sacrificing the chicken. But Lord Indra is covetous. He is not satisfied with food and drink. Finally, the forest man decides the method. On the old priest's advice, a part of the gazing field is cleaned, country liquor is drunk, and a portion is offered to Lord Indra. All of them take a sip, and then the damsels tuck a yellow flower behind the ear and dance so that Lord *Indra* can enjoy the beauty of their bare scud. The body of the damsel swings to the rhythm of the song. The cloud bursts, but it rains scantily as if Lord *Indra* has shown his kindness. The man of the forest mayn't understand anything but can understand that woman is the source of power. She is *Bhudevi*[2], and as the *Bhudevi* evoked so, *Indra* was scared.

Lord *Indra* showers a few drops of rain and creates an illusion, and the sun shines again through the clouds. In this belief and disbelief survives the man of the forest. He thinks that it's his fate, his destiny. He, in his state of faith,

2   Bhudevi- Goddess of Earth

can only presume. He doesn't know the ways to go against the fate. He understands that according to our deeds, we get the fruit. The branch of the *Karma tree*[3] *(Nauslea Parvifolia)* is then placed in the centre of the dancing arena and worshipped as a symbol of God and Nature. People worship the branches and seek the blessings of the *Karma Devata*. They dance to the tune of *Maadal (a popular tribal instrument* drum made of a hollowed tree trunk with *skins stretched at both ends)*, drink rice beer, sing and offer the drink to the Lord to make him happy.

> *Will sing Karmaa song, don't know the meaning;*
>
> *Bow down, bow down to you Karmaa Godmother*
>
> *Bestow your mercy on us oh Mother.*

What evil did they do? The Satan rain, instead of pouring, sprinkled a few drops like the grains for the birds, mocked at them and vanished on a horse. While leaving, leaves a few drops of rain like throwing a fistful of broken rice.

Clueless elderly people sitting on the veranda, think that it's the Dark Age *(Kaliyug)*. The young boys with dreams in their eyes get ready to go to different places, and the young girls leave the house and go somewhere and later are not traced. Young girls on weekly market days, go to the market for never to return and nobody knows where they are gone. The village damsel is lost. The young boy had promised to return in two months and never returns. Lord *Indra*, in the off-season, pours all his balance water on the mountain chests. The forest grows, but there is no farming. The creeper and bushes grow, but the people

---

3   Karma tree- This tree is the symbol of Karma Devata who is worshipped by tribal

leave the village. The villages become empty. Old people who can't even walk a few steps remain in the village. Just for this little rain, the man of the forest suffers.

He believes what he has not seen and doesn't trust whom he meets. He cannot weigh who is bigger- God or Government! Sometimes God is bigger, and Government is in some other time. In this calculation, he couldn't understand whom to ask for whom to beg. He gives spices, resin, gum, latex, timber, and wood and asks for salt, food, and clothes.

The government sends teachers, cereals, medicines, construct roads and connect electricity, nothing reaches them crossing the *Udanti* River. In the forest develops a hinterland. In contrast, the precious wood like *sal, gambhari, piasal and Indian rosewood* from the forest are taken away crossing the river. The tigers, bears and elephants vanish just like that. The wildlife becomes extinct, the army occupies the place, and instead of the roar of the tiger, the sound of the tanks can be heard. An India gets built inside the forest.

In this way, the forest recedes. People from nearby areas get reduced. Still, the clouds don't understand; people adhering to their fate don't understand, and the young generation exiting the villages with dreams in their eyes don't understand.

CHAPTER 7

Sarasi had a nasty headache when she woke up in the morning. She woke up from the mat and leaned on the wall. Why is she feeling heaviness in her head? Maybe she will get a fever. Sitting on the veranda, *Antaraa* heard the jingling sound of the bangles and said: Make some tea for me.

Sarasi pretended as if she didn't hear anything. There was a constant throbbing pain in her head. She remembered the incident that happened last night. She was angry with *Antaraa* and didn't eat properly and brought some rice beer of ten rupees from *Surukani* and drank it. She usually doesn't drink rice beer, but sometimes, to get rid of the tiredness after work, she drinks *Mahuli*. At a young age, she never drank country liquor. She still remembers that when she was hardly five years old, at that time, fifteen people in her village died drinking rice beer, and her father was one of them.

Sarasi's father rejected two proposals of *Sarasi* because they didn't serve him rice beer. He came back and said: They are poor and hungry. They don't have money for a drink; what will they feed my daughter? I visited their house, but they couldn't give me even five rupees to drink. They just offered me some useless drink.

Sanyaasi's father was robust and stout, with another young man carrying a dead buffalo on their shoulder to *Kisinda*. *Sarasi's* father had been to *Sidiga Guda* and saw them on the way. Being astonished, he paused for a few minutes, seeing two young guys lifting such a big dead buffalo and *Sarasi's* father asked *Sanyaasi's* father: Whose son, are you?

Sanyaasi's father laughed aloud like a joker and said: Are you going to get your daughter married to me?

: Useless fellow! whether I will give my daughter in your hands or not is a second thing, but tell me your father's name.

: Why? Do you want to be a friend of my father?

: Hey! Why are you mocking me?

The man accompanying the lift of the dead bullock smiled and said: Why are you arguing with him this way? Please, let us go. You want to know his father's name? *Nikas Satnemi* is his father's name, who died long back and is already a ghost. Do you have any work with him, dear?

: Where are you taking this dead bullock?

: To *BijuGuda,* our village.

After two days, Sarsai's father arrived at *Antaraa's* house. *Antaraa's* mother was sitting on the veranda, making brooms, and keeping an eye on the carcass kept for drying. *Sarasi's* father could immediately realize that it was the house of *Nikash Satnemi.*

: Is it the house of *Niksh Satnemi*?

The lady looked at the visitor in surprise as she heard her husband's name from someone after a long time. Who is this who is searching for *Nikas Satnemi*? Everyone in the village knew it was *Antaraa*'s house, and she was *Antaraa*'s mother.

: You are from which village? Do you have any work with my son?

: Is your son's name *Antaraa*? I saw him carrying the animal carcass on his shoulders. Your son is robust and stout.

Antaraa's mother was surprised. Who is this unknown man who has an eye on his son?

: Why do you have an eye on my son? Why are you saying so many things about my son?

Sarasi's father extinguished the bidi in his hand and hooked it on the eartop.

He said: Why are you so angry? Why should I have an eye on your son? I have come up with a marriage proposal.

: You are from which village? For whose daughter did you bring the proposal?

: My daughter.

: are you shameless! Why did you come on your own? Don't you have any relatives?

: Why are you angry? I was on my way to *SingidaGuda* and met your son.

: Ok, you may sit. I will call my neighbours and relatives. You can discuss it with them.

Sarasi heard everything from her father. He was praising *Antaraa*. He said he is very agile and robust and will work and earn. There won't be scarcity of anything in life.

Antaraa's mother came with her neighbours and relatives from *BijiGuda* and fixed the marriage. After a few months, she got married and came to Biju*Guda*. She could realize that *Antaraa* was really strong as he went to remote villages to collect the bones and animal carcasses to sell in *Rehman*'s storehouse. He was one of the most solicited leaders among *Satnemis*. The one who works and manages better will be the leaders among Satnemis.

The year *Sanyaasi* was born, he broke his leg. If he hadn't broken his legs, this situation wouldn't have arisen. Because of his leg, he couldn't walk, so *Sarasi* had to go to *Kisinda* daily. But there was one more reason for *Sarasi* to go to *Kisinda*. *Murshidabad* Muslims camp for two months in that area. At that time, they bargain and purchase old livestock. They take the livestock from grazing during the daytime. After the number of livestock increases, a group takes the livestock to *Calcutta, Malda* and *Murshidabad*. Along with the livestock, they also purchase bones and skin. Another group carry these in a truck and goes to their native places.

Nowadays, the number of Murshidabad Muslims has decreased. Hardly few of them come, and their income has also reduced. People have also reduced rearing livestock. In the villages, a few families barely keep a few cows in their sheds, and now, instead of the cows, more two-wheelers are seen in the villages.

Sarasi was suspicious about the Murshidabad Muslim boy. He had come to *Kisinda* that year, but he wasn't seen after that. Every year during this time, *Sarasi* goes in search of this boy. She could see the same old faces and a few more new faces but could never find that boy again. *Sarasi* asks about that boy to *Ahmeed, Harif and Liakat*, but they need to give information about it. The boy's name was *Murrad*, and he was the nephew of *Abubakur*. *Abaubakur* died in *Purulia* many years back because of dysentery while returning home. Others who were travelling with him did his last rites at that place. The old man had no son, so *Murrad* was everything to him.

Sarasi asked: Where is that *Murrad*?

Liakat surprisingly asked her: Do you some work with him?

: Tell me, where did he go? I will tell you why I am asking about him.

Liakat couldn't understand what *Sarasi* wanted to say. Still, he never wanted her to be sad, so he said: He crossed the border and went to Bangladesh.

: Where is that country? How far is it from our village? Why did he go to that country? How else went along with him?

: Why are you asking so many questions? Did you lend him some money?

: I am a poor lady, so where will I get the money to lend? I don't have enough to eat, but the boy has stolen something precious. To which country did he go? Where is he staying? How much money is required to go to that country?

: Do you want to go? Asks *Liakat* and laughs. Go from here. You are mad.

Sarasi got angry. She isn't insane. Why does everyone think her to be insane? Is it insanity to ask about her children? If so, then she is insane. She has four children, but now she doesn't know where they went.

She mockingly said: Yes, I have three children, and they are earning, and I am sitting and eating, isn't it? Look! I cannot arrange my own living, and I need to know in what condition my children will be.

: And your daughter?

: Where are my children? *Sarasi* said and started sobbing.

Antaraa was sitting on the veranda and was waiting for tea. He said in a raised voice: Are you dreaming during the daytime? I have a headache. Give me some tea.

Sarasi became conscious and thought she couldn't go to *Kisinda* that day as her head was reeling. She washed her face and cleaned the stove. Took the broom, swept the floor, and sprinkled some cow dung water in the courtyard. In the meantime, *Antaraa* got up from the veranda, came angrily towards her, and said: Can't you hear, or you don't care for what I say? I will give you a slap.

: You want to beat me? Beat. Why are you angry with me? Why didn't you beat the forest guard if you wanted to win? If you are a man in the true sense, hit the forest guard and show your masculinity.

Anara's ego was hurt. He rushed towards *Sarasi* and said: Do you want to see how I can beat them? *Antaraa* wasn't as strong as he used to be, but still, he punched *Sarasi*. She said: You scoundrel! Why are you beating me? What did I do? She pushed *Antaraa*, and he fell. His walking stick flung from his hand. *Sarasi*'s eyes were filled with tears, and she went near *Antaraa* and made him stand.

Though with the help of *Sarasi*, *Antaraa* could stand, he was still angry. He said: I will go to the town and beg but won't touch a single grain of food served by you. You are a whore, the kept of *Rehman*.

Sarasi couldn't tolerate it anymore. She hissed like a wounded serpent, rushed towards *Antaraa*, and said: Get lost, get lost from the house, or I will leave the house. I will swallow poison and die but will never step into your home. You are my husband, and you are mudslinging. She sat down, rebuked, and cried.

When I say it hurts you, do you know how the people in the village criticize and ridicule it? Do you say anything to them at that time? Why are you creating a scene early in the morning?

Sarasi said: Did you say anything different? Sita maa went through the fire test as Lord Rama had apprehension. She left the house. The outsiders will speak whatever they want and will ridicule, but when your own people believe in that, the heart bleeds.

Once there is a spot in the character, it can never go. All the good deeds go in vain. *Sarasi* had a headache since the morning but forgot about it after the incident. She felt as if this pain is more dreadful than the headache. She had thought that after completing the household chores, she would go to *Kisinda*. They are poor people, so to earn their living, she has to go despite her ill health, but after listening to the noxious words of *Antaraa*, she didn't feel like going. Just now, *Antaraa* has scolded her and said that she is the keeper of *Rehman*, so how can she go to her storehouse now? *Sarasi* works in *Rehman's* storehouse and takes care of the plants in his courtyard. She does whatever is told to her. What will they eat if she won't get the rice and the money?

She had decided that she won't go to *Kisinda*. It doesn't matter if there is anything to eat or not. When the man suffers from hunger, will he understand the difference between saying and doing? She brought a lump of mud and started coating the kitchen verandah. *Antaraa* had left the house after the quarrel. Suddenly *Sarasi* remembered that Liyakat was saying that a group from Murshidabad would arrive in *Kisinda*. A ray of hope shined in her heart regarding *Murrad*.

Murray may come along with that group, but if he goes to another village for some work? She completed her work quickly, prepared black tea, and saw *Antaraa* sitting on the verandah. She served him tea with some puffed rice and said: Take. I am going to *Kisinda*. I have to clean *Rehman*'s meat shop.

Antaraa still needs to reply to *Sarasi*. He sipped tea and ate puffed rice. While leaving the house, *Sarasi* said: There is some rice water. If you want, you can drink it.

Sarasi gave a long list of her work purposely to *Antaraa* as she wanted to hide from *Antaraa* that she was going to meet *Murrad* or maybe because of the quarrel in the morning. She left the house quietly, but there was hesitation when leaving. She was feeling helpless. After walking for some time, she felt a little better. It doesn't matter what *Sanyaasi*'s father thinks, but till she can work, she will search for her children, and one fine day, her family will be with her. She will have her children, grandchildren, and happiness in the house.

She will ask *Murrad* where did he take her daughter? He took her, but why didn't he bring her at least once to meet her mother? After three sons, she had a daughter. What will she be eating? How would she be a mother-in-law? She will ask him though he belongs to a different caste and religion, why did he love her daughter? Her daughter might be finding it difficult to adjust to the lifestyle of the Muslims. She imagined– *Murrad* wheedling away her daughter.

Sarasi reached *Kisinda* and, before going to *Rehman*'s storehouse, went to where the Muslims had set up their camp. *Liyakat* wasn't there. She sometimes speaks to him. *Harif* was cooking. *Sarasi* asked: *Dada*, we were supposed to come from your village. Did they come?

Harif said- yes. *Suleman* and *Saukat* have come.

: Only two of them?

: Why? Do you want anything? Did *Rehman* send you here?

: No. I was asking about that boy.

: You will go insane one day asking about Murad. Are you mad? Where will he take your daughter? We have yet to see your daughter along with him. Go back to your house.

: *Dada*, are you telling the truth?

: *Murrad* returned with us to *Murshidabad*, and from there, he crossed the border and went to his uncle's house. All of us know that.

: Then what about my *Parabaa*? Where did she go?

Harif couldn't give an answer to this question. He knew that it was not the work of his community.

Sarasi wasn't willing to accept this. It was a market day, and *Sarasi* was returning after completing her work in *Rehman*'s storehouse. She saw her daughter along with

Murray. Both were talking and giggling. When the boy saw *Sarasi*, he went away from there.

: What was that boy saying?

: Who?

: That Muslim boy.

: *Parabaa* became serious and told- About his village.

: Why were you laughing?

: What are you saying, Mother? *Parabaa* was angry.

Sarasi couldn't say anything immediately, but after some time, she said: Don't speak to those outsiders.

: Why?

: Because I am telling you not to speak to them.

: But all of them talk to you about. He is a good boy. See! What did he bring for me? She opened the knot in her saree and showed a pair of stone studded earrings.

: How much money is he asking for this?

Parabaa laughed and said- He won't take money for this.

Sarasi was apprehensive. She has only one beautiful daughter. *Sarasi* had a desire that she would get her daughter married to a good family. She will look for a groom for her daughter who can feed her properly, but when did her daughter become so friendly with the boy that she doesn't know. Doesn't matter if the groom does an office job, but he must earn two thousand rupees monthly. Nowadays, children don't do their ancestral business. They like people who are doing different types of business. They are also working in cities and in factories.

She snatched the artificial earrings from *Parabaa*'s hand and threw them. She said: *Parabaa*, will you not allow me to stay in the village? Your brother married into a different caste, so we had to leave the town. Are you going to do the same thing? How will your father feel when he comes to know about it? He will get you married immediately to someone. Who gave you this foolish idea? *Sarasi* was holding *Parabaa*'s hand and was dragging her as if she left her hand, then her daughter would elope with the Muslim boy.

On the way, she asked *Parabaa* many things. She asked: were you only speaking to him, or did you do anything else?

: What else will I do? *Parabaa* asked. *Sarasi* was mum. What answer will she give to this question? Both walked silently. Her mother was holding her hand tightly. *Parabaa* said: Leave my hand. *Sarasi* became conscious and held her slackly. She again asked: Where did that boy take you?

Parabaa didn't like her mother interrogating her. She didn't answer anything in anger.

: Did the boy take you to the forest or not?

: Why are you asking me unnecessary things? What would happen if I had been there?

: You have ruined yourself. Why did you do this?

: What did I do? Why are you scolding me?

Sarasi couldn't say anything. Is she blaming her daughter unnecessarily? She prayed: God! Nothing should happen to my daughter. She had dreams in her eyes and was saving money to purchase ornaments for her daughter's marriage. But she felt as if the girl would go out of her control.

Parabaa took long steps and moved ahead as if she didn't want to hear the scolding anymore. She is like a bird, and *Sarasi* can't cage her. *Sarasi* was calling: *Parabaa, Parabaa*, but could not run and hold her.

Parabaa reached home early and complained to her father. *Antaraa* loved the girl a lot. He could never see tears in his daughter's eyes. As soon as *Sarasi* reached home, he supported his daughter and started quarrelling with *Sarasi*. *Sarasi* kept quiet and didn't narrate the entire episode. She was scared that if *Antaraa* came to know, he would become outraged.

That day *Sarasi* understood that it's too difficult to become a mother. She kept an eye on her daughter but didn't know that her daughter would leave the house without anyone's knowledge. Since then, she has had a doubt about Murad. She could never forget that day but could never tell anyone.

: *Parabaa*, where did you go? She mused.

Sarasi went to *Rehman*'s vegetable garden and watered the plants. She saw the plants flowering. Near the fence were the flowering pigeon pea plants loaded with yellow flowers. The Moringa pods were hanging from the tree. After a few days, those will bear the pods. The other side of the fence was broken by someone, so if not repaired, then the cattle would enter and eat the vegetables. *Rehman* never took care of his vegetable garden. He had a small room next to it where he dumped the trash. When *Sanyaasi* eloped with Baiju Sara's daughter, *Sarasi* took shelter in that room.

As she was staying with her children, she cleaned the room and made it suitable for visiting. *Rehman* learned that the lady was very hardworking, so he told *Antaraa*: Instead of killing your time, clean the area, make a vegetable garden, and surround it with a fence.

The couple surrounded the small piece of land with a fence, levelled the soil, added manures, and bought seeds from the village market. A well near *Rehman*'s storehouse wasn't used for a long time. The couple cleaned the well and watered the plants. There was greenery in the garden. *Rehman* was happy the couple could make fertile pastureland and gifted them new clothes.

All the vegetables grown in the vegetable garden were sent to *Rehman*'s house. Though *Rehman* had a large family, the yield was enough for his family, and whatever was left out was used by *Sarasi*. Rice is a necessary part of the diet. But can only vegetables fill the stomach? She asked *Rehman*: Is there any work for me in the shop?

Rehman said: How can I provide you with work every day?

Sarasi said: There is no rice in the house.

Sometimes *Rehman* used to give her four to five rupees, but he couldn't pass every day. Still, *Sarasi* worked hard in the garden as she thought it was not the garden of *Rehman* but her. Sometimes she felt that the day she died, the garden would wither.

Sometimes if *Rehman* is in a good mood, he sits and speaks to *Sarasi* about life. He shows concern for his first wife, who couldn't get up from the bed. *Sarasi* says: *Dada*, inform your wife that I will come and give her an oil massage.

: You are stupid. Will my wife let you enter the house?

Sarasi nods her head and says: That's true.

Rehman asked: What about your elder son? Your son is educated but isn't caring for his parents. Do you have your grandchildren or not?

Whenever *Sarasi* hears this, her eyes brim with tears. She remembers her children, especially when she remembers her daughter *Parabaa* whose heart aches.

She thinks her sons will work and manage their living but what about her daughter? What will she be doing?

Rehman knew about *Sarasi*'s apprehensions. He says: Are you asking everyone about *Murrad*? That boy doesn't have anyone. Why are you after him?

Sometimes *Sarasi* suspects *Rehman*. *Rehman* has two wives, so if *Murrad* has made her daughter his second wife? If they won't feed their daughter correctly? *Sarasi* was restless. She shouted: *Parabaa*, my *Parabaa*, where did you go?

Sometimes Sarsi and her husband quarrelled, thinking about their daughter. They cry helplessly. To forget the pain and grief, she goes to *Surkani*. She purchases *Mahula*[4], and *Antaraa* goes to *Kalandar*'s rice beer shop.

Both come back home after drinking and crying. When the intoxication becomes more intense, *Antaraa* says: Look! The boys are going to the cities in search of work, and

---

4   Mahula: Mahua/ Mahula is a medium-sized decidu-
     ous tree. The sweet, fleshy flowers are eaten fresh or
     dried, powdered and cooked with flour, used as a
     sweetener, or fermented to make alcohol.

someone is stealing the town's young girls at night, and at dawn, it is found that few of the girls aren't there in the village. One day the village will be empty.

Sarasi asks: Who is stealing the girls at night?

Antaraa replies: Who knows? And then he goes to sleep.

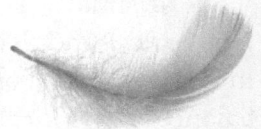

CHAPTER 8

Do you know *Krishna*? There is nothing called hell. Hell, and heaven are here. All of them are rewarded according to their deeds.

Krishna said: You are right. But what sin did we commit that we are suffering?

: Tell me, who doesn't commit a sin in this world? This world is fantastic. Doesn't hunger drive one to sin?

: Why did you remind me of hunger? If you don't think about desire, you are at peace, right? Krishna said this and left the pace. His house was in front of *Antaraa*'s house. He went and sat there and mumbled something.

Sometimes when *Antaraa* feels hungry or is disappointed, he recites a few lines from *Chautisa*[5] and *Bhaagawat*. As Krushna wasn't interested in listening to him and left so, to draw his attention, he repeated:

"One who drinks the ambrosia of the name of God

knows the fervour or tireless devotion."

Krishna was irritated listening to it and said: Well, enough. Be quiet.

---

5   Chautisa -a genre of literary composition in Indian literature. It was a popular form of writing in medieval poetry.

Krishna was suffering from Parkinson's disease. His hands and legs had unintended or uncontrollable movements, such as shaking, stiffness, and difficulty with balance and coordination. Maybe because of that, when *Antaraa* recited a few lines from the scriptures, his face reflected irritation. Why will he take the name of God when he isn't able to feed him one meal per day?

His head was shaking as if he was saying. No, no.. there is nothing in this world. There is no God, no peace, no one of your own. Whatever you see is just an illusion.

Antaraa sometimes thinks that all the people in the village are sinners. Like all the people in *Gopa* were saints in their previous birth, in a similar way, they were sinners in their final delivery. Like him, all of them have committed sins, and that's why they are all suffering. Other than people like *Surkani* and *Kalandar*, all of them are in pain.

He remembers the white-skinned man when he thinks about sin and sinners. Oh! What a pain? But could *Antaraa* free himself from the pain? Was it sin or saintly? When he goes to *Guru Haridas* ashram, he will ask *Ghana Das* Baba whether he committed a sin or something pious. Still, if a tiger devouring a deer is a sin, then he has done a sin.

After being in pain for a long time, his heart longed to go to *Guru Haridas's* ashram, but he was responsible for *Sarasi*. To whom will he give the responsibility of *Sarasi*?

Sarasi still has hope that one day her children will return. They aren't the chicks of the bird that, once they get the wings, will fly away forever. They are the children of human beings and will return to their birthplace. In insanity, *Sarasi* searches for her son Collector in the forest. She thinks the witch has kept her son *Sanyaasi* in a stony cave and shouts *Sanyaasi, Sanyaasi* loudly. *Antaraa* tries to wipe out the *Mem*ories of the days they had spent with their children in *Kisinda* in the small room provided by *Rehman* from *Sarasi's* mind, but the *Mem*ories are unforgettable.

In search of the girl, *Sarasi* walks five kilometres daily to *Kisinda* even though she doesn't have work in *Rehman's* storehouse. People try to make her understand, but she can never understand and thinks *Murrad* has taken her daughter away. Sometimes *Antaraa* also feels the same. They have often considered registering a complaint with the police. Still, he fears the police and the police station. Does he have enough money to fight the case?

Before leaving the village, the boy worked as a helper in *Bila Sing's* truck, earned some money, and said that he would learn how to drive a car in a month as he had spoken to the driver to teach him. The driver said he would arrange a license by taking fifteen hundred rupees. He worked as a helper for a year. At night, Bila Singh's truck used to enter the forest, load the logs, and deliver it to a go down at *Nuapada*. *Daaktar* used to visit the house once a week. Whenever *Antaraa* looked at his well-built physic, he remembered his youth. He could imagine himself in his place. His nature, physic, and qualities matched *Antaraa*. The boy was always happy. The day he got his salary, he bought clothes for his siblings, utensils for his mother, a towel and some bidis for his father.

He behaved like a mature person. He kept a part of his earning, and the rest he gave to his mother.

Surprisingly, he got into the trap of the forest guard. He was seen every time along with him. He took a cigarette from him and smoked, and the boy who never drank was always seen in *Kalandar's* shop. *Antaraa* could no longer tolerate it. How long can he let an earning family *Member* leave his job and sit idle at home? One day he asked him: You are supposed to learn to drive. What happened?

Daaktar didn't answer.

: Where is the license?

: Can you give me fifteen hundred rupees to take out a permit?

: What did you do with the money that you earned? If you don't work, how can you earn fifteen hundred rupees? Tell me, why did you leave work?

: Father, why are you after me?

: The forest guard has spoiled you.

: Why are you blaming him? Bila didn't give me the money and said – You Wanker!

The son of a *Chamaara*, you thief, get out of here.

: Why did he address you as a thief? Did you steal anything?

: What did I steal? I don't know anything, Father. It is his way of talking. He said you are a *Chamaara*, and how dare you enter my house? He told me to deliver the goods, and I went. What is my mistake?

: What are the things that you provided?

: It's not what you are thinking, Father. He told me that I had stolen timber.

: Why?

: His driver gave wood to the Dhaba owner without anyone's knowledge. What did I do? Is Bila, not a thief who is stealing timbers from the forest?

: All of them stole, then why did he say you as a thief?

: Are you the police? Why are you interrogating me like police?

: It's not like that. The driver sold timbers, then instead of the driver, why did he beat you?

: The driver is a clever person. He said to Bila that he was drunk, so he told me to look after the timbers, and after that, he didn't know what had happened.

Antaraa said: Why did Bila believe what he said? How did he trust? How could you take out such big pieces of logs? Let's go to Nuapada and tell him. I will plead with him to keep you in the work.

: If you do that, then I will leave the house.

: Why are you behaving insanely?

Antaraa was nervous as he heard his son threatening him. Whose evil eyes are on his family? He was trying to forget the pain of Collector leaving the house, but will *Daaktar* also leave the house? He wasn't ready to believe it. He felt as if there was some other reason.

Antaraa remembered that Doctor purchased a watch and a pair of shoes a few days back. He also bought a tape recorder to listen to the songs. He never thought about where he got so much money. Instead, was happy and, as his son, was successful. His son also said that he would purchase a bicycle. His mother told him to buy the bike later and give her the money to repair the house's roof.

Did his son steal? Is it true what *Bila Singh* said? Still, *Antaraa* couldn't accept it. He thought that all his children had the traits of their mother. They can't deceive anyone.

They can die but will never steal. The driver was a shrewd person who trapped his son in this matter.

Why does it always happen to him? He dreamt many things about Collector, but the boy left the village and went to the city. He can't imagine how he would look, and maybe he won't be able to recognize him. He thought that *Collector* would change the situation of his house, but that has yet to happen. *Daaktar* was also working hard and earning well. He could have changed the position of the house in a year, but that didn't happen.

Antaraa could climb the mountain at a young age and walk to distant places. *Rehman* trusted him as whatever he told *Antaraa* did perfectly. He did all the work entrusted to him to earn more. In the evening, when *Antaraa* returned home, *Sarasi* kept the house clean and sat eagerly waiting for him. He said: Don't you have any other work besides cleaning the house?

: You are saying about work. Do we have enough grains in the house that I will be busy cleaning?

: Go and get me some water. I am thirsty. *Sarasi* brought water for him in a glass. *Antaraa* gave his mother the money he had earned, cleaned his feet, and entered the house. Sometimes he bought glass bead necklaces and some sweets for *Sarasi*. He jokingly asks *Sarasi*: Would you have eaten so many sweets if you had married someone else?

Sarasi makes a crooked face and says: Why didn't you bring a saree for me? The saree that she was wearing was almost torn. Though *Antaraa* worked like an ox still, he could never arrange money to purchase a saree for *Sarasi*. To make *Sarasi* happy, he said: I will bring it for you next time from *Kisinda*. Will I feel good if you become angry?

His son earned more than him. He could purchase clothes for his siblings and also a watch for himself. Happiness and sadness are a part of life. Happiness doesn't remain for a long time, so it happened to him, also.

If it's not a sin, then what's it? That day while returning from *Rehman*'s storehouse, he saw the weekly market. He wanted to avoid purchasing vegetables, mustard or *mandia* (Millet) **as** it wasn't required. He wanted to buy a saree. There were a few vendors who were selling sarees. *Antaraa* went to one of them and selected a red saree with yellow flowers printed on it and bargained for it. Finally, he bargained it for fifty rupees. He looked at his pocket pouch and found that he didn't have fifty rupees. He couldn't purchase the saree, and the market timing got over.

After a few days, while returning from *Lephrikhola*, he saw a cow. He walked towards it. What is it? Whose is it? God has listened to his prayers. He remembered the saree he had selected for *Sarasi*.

Still, *Antaraa* remembers that day. He was happy, thrilled, and excited. He thought for a while and left the place. After reaching home, he felt that does anyone forgo fortune. He became sad looking at *Sarasi*. If he had brought the dead cow, he could have purchased many more sarees for *Sarasi*. The saree would have looked good on *Sarasi*.

Sarasi realized that *Antaraa* was mumbling something. What has happened to him? Did she do anything wrong by asking him for a saree? He is poor and works hard to feed his family and take care of the house. He could have given a saree at his convenience. *Sarasi* asked: What are you thinking? Why are you looking so pale?

Antaraa replied and left the house. He was repenting. He thought, what would have happened? What would I feel? Will that still be there waiting for him? He had acted foolishly. Who leaves the things in hand?

It was almost dark by that time. In deep remorse, he went to *Kalandar's* shop and said: *Kalandar*, give me a glass of rice beer. Here is the money. You can give me a bottle.

: Did you earn enough money today?

: *Antaraa* was startled as if his secret was known. He fumbled. He controlled himself and said: Give me. Why are you asking so many things? How much do I earn? Earned is divided among five to six people when a dead animal is carried.

As *Kalandar* got the money so he gave him the liquor. If someone takes a bottle, then he makes more profit. He gave the bottle, along with a few chickpeas, to *Antaraa*. *Kalandar*

He kept separate bottles for the cameras as he believes in caste, but as he has the liquor shop, he will be at a loss if he thinks about the caste.

Antaraa could neither enjoy the drink nor the spiced chickpea that day as he was repenting at his foolishness. He returned home in gloominess.

Though drunk that day, he still couldn't sleep properly that night. He was restless. And after some time, he fell asleep. But before dawn, he woke up. *Sarasi* was still sleeping. *Antaraa* came outside. Still, there wasn't enough sunlight outside, and his mother sat and dozed on the veranda. She saw *Antaraa* going out early in the morning and asked: Where are you going so early? Won't you have tea?

He said: I will come back just now.

From *BijuGuda* to *Lephriphal* is hardly four kilometres. Many thoughts and apprehensions surrounded him on the way. Will that corpse be there or not? It was near the bush in the forest. By the time it was sunrise, he was already near the frontier. He could see the animal still lying under the tree from a distance. There was a smile on *Antaraa*'s lips. He walked towards the animal rapidly and sat down on the ground. No, it's still alive. It was lying under the tree with legs spreadeagled with a fixed stare in its eyes, and the flies covered its face. Its left leg sometimes quivered, indicating it was still alive. *Antaraa* took out a small box from his waist pouch, which had the power of the hemp plant, and kept it in his mouth. After some time, he spat and said: Why are you still alive? Die, die. For you, I couldn't sleep at night. *Antaraa* took out a bidi and kept it between his lips, and suddenly, he remembered that he didn't have the matchbox with him. Where will he get the fire to light the bidi? He kept the bidi back.

He touched the animal carefully. This time the right leg also quivered. He said: Why are you not dying? If you want to die, then die quickly; otherwise, how long will I wait for you to die? I will press your neck, and all your drama will be over.

The next moment *Antaraa* was a little scared. Will he commit a sin because of his greediness? How can he take the life of such a big animal? Though he has eaten the flesh, he has never hunted any animal. *Antaraa* muffled. *Antaraa* is a non-vegetarian, but he has never killed a cow. In his caste, many of them kill the cows, but he doesn't as he thinks it is sacred. He had no way out except to wait for the cow to die.

Whose cow, is it? Why is the owner not searching

for it? If it had been a snake bite, the fluid must ooze out from the mouth, but it wasn't as such. There were only two streams of tears rolling down from its eyes. Ah! What is the animal suffering from? What will happen if the owner comes and see *Antaraa* sitting next to it like a death angel? He will scold and beat him. But the animal is still not dead. *Antaraa* got up and checked the breath of the animal. It was alive.

Suppose the cow dies, then how will he carry it alone? If he calls his neighbours, then they will ask for money. He couldn't leave the animal and go as at any time it may die. If it dies, then after a few days, the body will decompose, the foul smell will spread, and his neighbours will come to know.

Antaraa was in a fix. He broke the tree branches and covered the animal with them so the outsiders couldn't see.

He had covered the cow with so many leaves and branches that it wasn't visible outside. But still, the animal is alive, so if he hides it like this, he might be caught. If the owner comes, then won't he be caught?

Antaraa knew that the corpse won't give a foul smell immediately. If the animal dies, then people will come to him to clean the place. He was confused between sin and good deeds, truth and falsity. Can he forgo his dignity and be called a thief? No, it can't happen. Suddenly he picked up a big stone, cleared the branches and leaves from the face of the animal and said- Your life is harrowing. I relieve you from that. He hit the face of the animal with the stone. It shook and became still.

After hitting it with a stone, *Antaraa* sat down silently as if he had killed a human. All his strength and courage vanished; he was sweating profusely. He has skinned many animals, plucked the horns from their head, cut the flesh, and dried it in his house under the sun, but he had never become so weak mentally. He regretted his deed. He thought it would have been alive if he had given it some water or treatment, but what did he do? For his own selfish intention, he killed the innocent animal.

He felt as if he is neck-deep in sin. Maybe Saturn has entered his mind. He remembered what his mother said- If there is a little mistake, Saturn enters, and if it enters, it engulfs the human. Mother also says that when Saturn overpowers, a human loses his power of thinking, and no difference remains between a Brahmin and Sudra.

Antaraa was standing on a rock. He had covered the dead cow with branches and leaves of the tree. He thought: Why is he so upset? Is there any difference between the life of a big animal and an insect? Is it so that if you kill an insect, it's not a sin, and if you kill a big animal, it's a sin? The cow was in pain, and he helped it to be free from the pain. Why are these unnecessary thoughts? *Antaraa* removed the box filled with hemp plant powder and kept a pinch in his mouth. He thought that he had to take the corpse from there. He needs a helping hand, but whom will he call so the incident doesn't come to light. All the people of his community are hungry, but he won't tell them. He will throw the flesh as the cow might suffer from any disease or be bitten by a snake. He won't call anyone for help. He was still thinking about the red and yellow printed saree. If still any money is left, then he will purchase anklets. He will prove to *Sarasi* that her husband is capable.

Antaraa returned home, and *Sarasi* was surprised to see his pitiless face. Where did he go early in the morning?

Why is he behaving insane, and what has happened to him? But before she could ask, *Antaraa* said: Is there anything to eat? At that time, *Sarasi* was eight months pregnant. She couldn't walk or do things properly. *Antaraa* said: You can sit down. I will go and check what is there to eat.

Sarasi didn't listen to him. She served him a big bowl of water rice with ground garlic pods and chillies. She asked him: Where did you go early in the morning? What has happened to you?

: Nothing has happened to me. He thought: His wife will deliver soon, so why did he commit a sin? If God blesses them, everything will be good with *Sarasi*. He prayed to God that *Sarasi* shouldn't suffer for his sin.

Antaraa said: If you have any money with you, please give me.

Sarasi had saved some money for the baby to be born. If it had been some other time, she would have never given the amount to him, but as he looked tensed and worried, *Sarasi* took out two rupees and gave him.

Antaraa left quickly with the bag, which contained all his tools. *Sarasi* looked at him in surprise, as the man had never left the house without informing her. What has happened? Who else is going along with him? *Sarasi* wanted to ask, but she couldn't.

When *Antaraa* was purchasing bidi from *Nurisa*'s shop, *Chamuri* saw him. He had come there to buy rice. *Antaraa* thought that he should ask *Chamuri* to accompany him as it differed from a single person's work. Still, if *Chamuri* informed others, no one would take him along with them in the future for any job. He has committed the sin, and why should others take the money?

He must again walk for five kilometres. Now the animal won't be in pain. It had suffered a lot of pain. He must skin the animal before sunset. He walked briskly. The dead corpse was still there, covered with the leaves and branches. He removed the covering and then started his work. It wasn't an old cow; it could have survived if treated with the herbs.

Antaraa carefully cut the hide and thought that he would sell that to *Rehman* for three hundred rupees. He will sell the horn to the craftsman at *Titilagad*, and after the flesh decomposes, he will think about whom to sell the bones to. He couldn't do the calculation but felt like he had become wealthy.

When he was cutting the hide, he came to know that the knife wasn't that sharp. He rubbed the blade on a stone and carefully started cutting the leather. He thought the animal would have run away if it had been alive, but now he is skinning it.

By the time he skinned the animal, it was almost evening. He thought that he would dig a pit and bury the corpse there so that when the body decomposed then, the foul smell won't circulate in the air. But what can he do at night? He didn't have the spade to dig the ground, and as it was evening, the mosquitoes also started biting. How can he leave the work in between and go to *Kisinda* or to his village? He felt helpless. Then he collected a few dry leaves and branches and lit the fire. He thought he would spend the night there; otherwise, all his efforts would be in vain. But if he stays in the forest at night, *Sarasi* will look for him and ask his neighbours. They will come to know. Why did he do this out of greediness?

He didn't have any other way. He looked for a ditch,

pulled the corpse, threw it there, and then covered the place with leaves and branches of the tree. It was difficult for him to hide such a giant corpse, and the flesh looked red. He thought that he was in trouble. He believes that he couldn't leave the animal this way, but if he went home and came back, it would give rise to suspicion. Instead, it would be good to spend the night there. In the morning, he can bury the corpse and carry the skin to *Kisinda*. But will he take the skin to his village or *Kisinda*?

He lit the fire and sat down though he was scared. He again thought that if he had cared for the animal, it would have survived. He has committed sin out of greediness. He sat there repenting. For the whole night, a corpse and a living person were together. He dozed and dreamt about the animal with eyes filled with tears, asking: Why did you kill me?

Antaraa was speechless. The animal again asked: Why did you kill me? My calf will be searching for me.

Antaraa was stunned. The animal was asking again and again: Why did you kill me….?

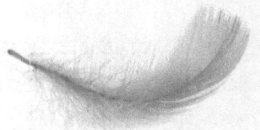

CHAPTER 9

*E*dital brought her close to *Sanyaasi* and was also responsible for taking him away from him. *Chaiti* thinks *Edital* is accountable for everything. Her *Sanyaasi* draws and is a drawing teacher in the missionary school. *Chaiti* is also very good at drawing, and she learnt it from her grandfather. She could pull the animals, birds, witches and many more. *Sanyaasi* says: Jesus Christ has brought us together. He mocks and says: You will become my teacher; that's why we met. I have you because of the music I played on my flute. At that time, I never knew that a girl in a red frock would come and stand in front of me like a mysterious goddess and would be attracted by the music of my flute. Do you remember how you came and stood before me and vanished suddenly? I searched for you and reached the group of stone cutters.

Chaiti laughs and says: I don't understand what you speak.

: It's better if you need help understanding. You remain as innocent as you are.

She taught *Sanyaasi* how to draw *Edital* pictures which she learnt from her grandfather. Her grandfather often fought with her father, saying – You are born to be a stone cutter, but why are you making my granddaughter cut the stones. Look at her hands.

Chaiti taught *Sanyaasi* to draw pictures like peacocks, parrots and many more. *Sanyaasi* was very good at drawing, so he could immediately follow her instructions and draw. She holds herself responsible for her husband being away from her in another country.

Sometimes *Chaiti* thinks it would have been better if she had only learnt to cut the stones and wouldn't have learnt *Edital* from her grandfather. If she wouldn't have taught *Sanyaasi*, then what would have happened? Why did she teach him? This is the reason why her husband is away from her. She sometimes blames herself and *Edital*[6].

One day Emanuel *Sahib*'s wife, Marina *Mem Sahib*, called for *Sanyaasi* in the evening. *Sanyaasi* always listens to *Mem Sahib*, so it doesn't matter if he has worked or is late at night; he immediately goes. He says: *Chaiti*, she was my mother at my previous birth. Because of her, I can earn today and live a respectful life; otherwise, think about how my life would have been?

After staying for many years in the Mission, it seemed as if *Sanyaasi* remembered his village and the colloquial language. He spoke in a refined speech, so *Chaiti* thought that *Sanyaasi* had become more intelligent and that whatever he was saying was for good. Who is responsible for the change in *Sanyaasi*? Non other than *Mem Sahib*. That's why whenever *Mem Sahib* calls for *Sanyaasi*, she never restricts him but instead says: Go, your mother is calling.

She was converted to Christianity in the church to marry *Sanyaasi*. That day, *Mem Sahib* told her to change her name from *Chaiti* to Isabella. The father of the church

---

6   Edital- Bohemian art

blessed *Chaiti* as Isabella, and after two days, Isabella married Christopher Satnemi. But she couldn't accept the new name so easily. Once, *Sanyaasi* jokingly called Isabella; Isabella listened to me. *Chaiti* was cutting the vegetables. She was engrossed in her thoughts and didn't hear. *Sanyaasi* came and shook her and said: I have been calling you for a long time. Are you not able to attend? Have you become deaf, or are you thinking about someone?

Chaiti asked: When did you call me? How could it be that I couldn't hear you? Are you telling the truth?

: You didn't hear Isabella; why didn't you hear Isabella?

Chaiti laughed to her heart's content and said- If you call me by the name which *Mem Sahib* has given, then how can I hear? I need to remember what is your name.

: Christopher

: Christopher and Isabella. *Chaiti* laughed loudly. Finally, you made me a Christian.

Sanyaasi said: No, *Chaiti*, we aren't Christopher and Isabella. We are the same *Sanyaasi* and *Chaiti* who belong to that village.

But *Sanyaasi* became Christopher Satnemi, went to a foreign country, and forgot *Chaiti*. Marina *Mem Sahib* isn't there; otherwise, she would have asked her about *Sanyaasi* and would have told her to give her back her *Sanyaasi*.

Marina *Mem Sahib* is *Sanyaasi*'s mother. Marina *Mem Sahib* gifted her a beautiful saree and some jewellery during their marriage. Can anybody else other than my mother do this? For *Sanyaasi* she bought a shirt, trousers, and shoes. Both exchanged the ring, and *Sanyaasi* looked like a *Sahib*.

Mem Sahib took the photographs with her camera, and in the Mission, she hosted a party. Could it have been done so grandly in the village? Merina *Mem Sahib* only gives some people a ring, shirt, trousers, or shoes. *Sanyaasi* is like her son, so whenever she calls, *Sanyaasi* goes.

Once, Emanuel *Sahib* said, few of them are visiting from foreign countries, so paintings will be done on the auditorium wall. It is the largest auditorium in Bhopal, and the entire wall will have *Edital* paintings. Each division will take a week to paint. *Sanyaasi* was given the responsibility of completing the work. *Sanyaasi* used to leave the house at 8 'O clock in the morning and return late in the evening. *Chaiti* was worried; other than that, she felt lonely alone. When *Sanyaasi* is at home, time passes swiftly, but now she is alone and feels disgusted.

As soon as *Sanyaasi* returned, she said: Don't go anymore. I feel lonely without you. Did you understand?

: How can it be? I still need to complete the work, and the delegates will arrive.

Sanyaasi was extremely tired and irritated by what *Chaiti* said. He said: Do you think I feel good about slogging like this? I am not in proper health and in pain because of too much work. Rather than understanding my pain, you are quarrelling with me.

There were tears in *Chaiti*'s eyes. She said: I will ask your mother why she makes you work hard and gives you so much pain?

Once *Sanyaasi* told her: Come and let us work together so we can complete the work quickly. If I can finish it early, then I need not go there.

Chaiti quivered as she listened to *Sanyaasi*. She said: Why? I can draw a few pictures at home, but I will still go and work in the office. Don't tell me all those things.

Chaiti thought that *Sanyaasi* would agree with what she said. But *Sanyaasi* was insistent. He said: You are my teacher, and people will appreciate your work. You have magic in your hands; if you go, everyone will enjoy your work. Will you come with me tomorrow?

Chaiti thought that *Sanyaasi* was joking, as she never thought that *Sanyaasi* solemnly wanted to take her along with him. But soon, she realized that *Sanyaasi* had tried to take her to the auditorium she shuddered. She felt feverish and thought of leaving the house, but how could she go to *Sanyaasi*? Who is there except *Sanyaasi*? People of her community and neighbours will rebuke her and vex her by asking puzzling questions. Who else other than *Sanyaasi* can give her so much love and respect?

At night *Chaiti* wasn't well and felt exhausted as she had dysentery. He went to the Mission hospital and brought medicines, but after taking the medication also, it didn't stop, and *Chaiti* was listless. *Sanyaasi* was surprised and was unable to understand why it happened.

He asked: What did you eat today?

: I will take you to the hospital.

: Hospital? They will give me an injection, so I won't go. Why are you troubling me?

: Am I bothering you, or are you bugging me? Let me see how to send the information to the Doctor.

: I will instead prefer to die here than go to the hospital. *Chaiti* started crying. *Sanyaasi* couldn't understand how to convince her. Just because of the fear of injection, she is inviting death. How can he leave her alone and call the Doctor and finally he said: I am tired. I can't do anything anymore.

Towards midnight *Chaiti* felt a little better and slept. *Sanyaasi* also slept, and when he woke up in the morning, he couldn't find *Chaiti*. He looked for her and found her drying her wet hair after a bath. She asked him: Will you not go to school today?

: I will go. How are you feeling now?

Chaiti said: Feeling better.

Sanyaasi completed his daily routine and was ready to leave. Both of them sat together and had breakfast. When they were in the village then, they didn't know what breakfast was, but life in a city was different. In the morning -breakfast, afternoon - lunch, evening- snacks and dinner. *Chaiti* never had the habit of eating three to four times a day. It wasn't a habit as there wasn't enough food at home to eat so many times, and it was like a dream for them.

Sanyaasi was ready to leave, and before that, *Chaiti* was near the doorway, draped in a saree. *Sanyaasi* was surprised. *Chaiti* could understand it and answered: Why are you looking at me in this way? I will also go and help you in your work.

Sanyaasi said: Don't go, as you aren't well. I was just joking. It's better if you take a rest. Cook for yourself and eat something and don't wait for me.

No, no, I will go. It's better to finish the work as soon as possible.

Sanyaasi never wanted to take his wife to work in the auditorium, but *Chaiti* insisted and went along with him.

There were many people in the auditorium. *Chaiti* was feeling a little shy, and the people there were surprised to see *Chaiti* and *Sanyaasi*.

Chaiti saw that half of the wall was designed, but those pictures could have been more lively. *Sanyaasi* couldn't draw like her grandfather. She was unhappy to see those pictures. She thought *Sanyaasi* had taken up such an extensive assignment but had made mistakes. The bows of the *Shabar*[7] (tribal man) could have been finer. Lines and the mouth of the dog. It would have looked beautiful if it had been a little more open. The dog's tail shouldn't have been near the mouth of the other dog, but she couldn't say anything to *Sanyaasi* in front of so many people. She could understand that *Sanyaasi* hadn't put all his efforts into drawing the pictures. He could have imagined the pictures before drawing as she couldn't find the reflection of creativity in those. Can the pictures be drawn if the painter doesn't imagine and isn't creative?

Sanyaasi introduced *Chaiti* to *Shridharan*. He wanted to avoid *Chaiti*, but *Sanyaasi* said: She would draw in one-fourth of this wall. Shridhar looked at *Sanyaasi* and gave a glance of disapproval as if he couldn't trust *Chaiti*. He said: We can't take the risk.

Sanyaasi said: Sir, she is my teacher, and I have learnt from her. Sridharan smiled and said: Let's see.

Chaiti held the brush and the colour palate after many days. After a long time, she was going to draw, and if

---

7   **Sabar-** Shabar and Saora are one of the of the Adivasi of Munda ethnic group tribe who live mainly in Odisha and West Bengal

her grandfather had been there, he would have been happy thinking that his granddaughter would finally use her skills. The colour was made by crushing the stones. The trees were in a row, followed by peacocks and parrots, and the dhangadaas had broad shoulders and thinner waistlines.

Sridharan was watching *Chaiti* drawing on the wall from a distance. He could see a depiction of a civilization. He was enchanted, as if someone was creating specific notes by putting pressure on the frets and the humans in the picture were alive.

: Wonderful.

Sanyaasi smiled and said: I already told you she is a good painter.

In the afternoon, *Sanyaasi* took *Chaiti* to the canteen near the auditorium. There was an office next to the hall, and the office employees were having their lunch in the canteen. *Chaiti* felt shy and uncomfortable, as if she had entered a prohibited area. She said: Let's go as I can't sit and eat here among so many people.

: Will you remain hungry?

: Let's go and have food outside in any other place.

: Who will go now? Don't behave like a child. Nothing will happen as I am there. Who is watching you in this place?

Chaiti sat on a chair cautiously.

: *Sanyaasi* asked: What do you want to eat?

: I will eat whatever you want to eat.

: You let me know as we aren't going to pay for what we eat. Do you want to eat chicken? Look! I have this pass, so we will eat for free whatever we eat.

: Every day?

: No. Are we going to work here every day.? Won't we go home?

As *Chaiti* was shy so she couldn't say what to eat. Somehow, she managed to eat something and left the place. She felt good after coming outside.

Both again went to the auditorium to draw. It was a new experience and excitement for *Chaiti*. Though she felt shy and scared, she enjoyed it. The city people recognize the talent of a human being, but who remembers the talent in the village? Does anyone in the town appreciate and say it's a beautiful painting? In the beginning, when she came to the city, she felt lonely and lamented, felt as if she was a prisoner. But now she feels comfortable in this life.

In the evening few people arrived, and Emanuel *Sahib* and Marina *Mem Sahib* were along with them. They spoke in English and sometimes, in between, spoke in Hindi. *Chaiti* understood that they were comparing the pictures she drew, and *Sanyaasi* drew. They were saying that *Chaiti's* drawings were more beautiful.

Chaiti and *Sanyaasi* were busy as they thought they would complete the drawings that day. They weren't bothered about someone praising or criticizing them, nor were they part of onlookers. They were innocent tribal people with dreams in their eyes to build a nest, absorbed in the rhythm of music regardless of the surrounding.

The work was almost complete, and it was night when they returned home. *Chaiti* was tired, and she could understand how stressful it would have been for *Sanyaasi* all these days, but as she stayed home alone, she was perturbed. While returning home, *Chaiti* said: It could be better to do so much work. If there had been time, I would have seen the garden you care for.

Chaiti didn't have the patience to cook rice. *Sanyaasi* said: Let's go and have our food in the hotel.

Chaiti said: I am not hungry. You can go and have food.

Sanyaasi was tired. He was engrossed in drawing, so he forgot everything, but now he felt as if he hadn't slept for ages. On the way, they bought a chat from the roadside stall and ate.

After reaching home, *Sanyaasi* said: Today you went outside to work, and you were praised, but if you had been there at home, would you have been praised? Didn't people say that your drawings were more beautiful than mine?

: What will I get from that? Will I compete with you? Are you different from me?

: No, no, I do not envy you. I was happy when people praised you.

: Are you telling the truth? *Chaiti* smiled and said: What is that which is in my tummy?

Sanyaasi couldn't understand what she meant to say. Later from the smile on *Chaiti*'s face, he could realize that he was going to be a father and was excited.

: Why did you go to work in this condition and only ate a plate of rice for the whole day? It's not good at all. Let me cook something for you. Why did you keep it a secret from me for so many days?

Both were happy. Though he was angry with *Chaiti* for her carelessness, but he was excited. Both got involved in lovemaking. Lovemaking is gratification.

Sanyaasi pulled *Chaiti* towards his chest.

Chaiti said: You only played the flute for a short time.

Sanyaasi said: I will take leave for a day, and we will go to the forest, and I will play the flute.

: Oh!

: I am alive for that; otherwise, I would have died long back.

: Is it true? What do you dream of?

: Many things. Like a house in the forest where my parents and your parents will stay. There are neighbours all around.

As if someone had opened the door of her closed room. Within that darkness of spider nets, within the rotten smell, lies her childhood days. There was a sense of freedom as the *Mem*ories of childhood came alive. *Chaiti* took a deep breath and exhaled. In her despair, breath mingled with someone else's breathing. Both were trying to understand the existence of each other in each other's arms as if they were two people floating in the river current.

CHAPTER 10

Parabaa was sitting and drawing lines on the ground with her nails. *Jhumuri* was in the house along with her regular customer. The beetle shop owner comes at least once or twice a week. Sometimes *Parabaa* thinks it's inappropriate to say that the man is a customer of *Jhumuri* rather than it can be said that *Jhumuri* is his beloved paramour because the man doesn't go to anyone else other than her. There is no bargain related to the money between them. Whatever he has, he gives and maybe sometimes more and sometimes less.

Jhumuri is beautiful and fair. She belongs to *Ganjam*, so she wears a nose pin, which suits her. Whenever the beetle shop owner comes, he brings beetle for *Jhumuri*. From that, *Jhumuri* gives one or two to *Parabaa*, which tastes good. *Jhumuri* sometimes borrows money from him if she wants to buy a saree or needs more cash to pay the rent. Sometimes he owed money to *Jhumuri*. Once he said: Today, I purchased a bicycle for my son, so I will give you money next time.

Parabaa couldn't understand whether it would be called conjugal life or friendship. No, it can't be called marital life. Instead, can be called friendship. But if it is friendship, then why does he pay money for sex?

Though *Parabaa* stays there still, the man never looks at her. *Parabaa* doesn't have any specific customer on whom she can rely in need other than that it is the place for prostitution, so whoever is more skilled, more beautiful customers visit them. *Parabaa* is like a person standing in the last row of the competition. If *Jhumuri* hadn't been there, it would have been difficult for her to survive. *Parabaa* isn't fit for this profession.

There was a change in *Jhumuri*'s behaviour as if she no more wanted to take responsibility for *Parabaa*. It was apparent as it was difficult for her to manage the responsibility, and she wanted *Parabaa* to care for her own things.

Jhumuri was also not happy as after *Kundaa* arrived, *Parabaa* often went to meet her, and sometimes *Kundaa* also visited their shack during business hours. *Jhumuri* thinks that as they belong to the same community, they have a good friendship. Sometimes *Jhumuri* waits for *Parabaa* to have food together, but she returns after having food with *Kundaa*. She thought *Parabaa* to be innocent and helped her, but now she behaves like *Kundaa*'s elder sister.

Jhumuri and *Parabaa* constructed a concrete wall between the room, covered the roof with polythene, and hung a curtain made from the old saree on the doorway. In the beginning, *Parabaa* felt a little uncomfortable as whatever they talk could be heard, but now she is used to it. *Parabaa* welcomes people from all age groups. She lies down like a gunny sack, impassive and cold. She stretches herself as an insensate lump of flesh. She allows her customers to abrade and stain with body fluids, not protesting the pain she is going through. As if she wanted to say: She has turned into a barren land,

and her feelings have eventually disappeared. She is like a wasteland, abject, ruthless, and impetuous, waiting for a drop of rain for ages.

Sometimes on a rainy night, when *Parabaa* listens to the chirping sound of the cricket, she remembers her village. She closed her eyes and saw her mother's face glowing in the light of the oil lamp. All of them sat near the hearth with their plates and served porridge. Mother says: It's hot, so have it quickly. Having hot rice with mashed garlic during the rainy season is most satisfying. After eating, covering oneself with a quilt and listening to the pitter-patter of the raindrop is enchanting.

Once mother fell sick during the rainy season in the month of *Shravan* . She suffered for a few days as she had an intermittent fever and couldn't go to *Kisinda*. It was raining heavily, and it didn't stop. Father sat in the house nit-picking. Just a year back, her younger brother fought with her father, left the village, and joined the Naxals. He wasn't on good terms with his father. When their father used to tell him about *dharma, karma* (action) and *karma phala*(the result of action), he used to get annoyed. He said: Why do you take the name of God? What has he given you? There is nothing called God. The village will change when people like *Nurisa, Alekha Pradhan*, and *Chudamani Nayak* are absent. Father doesn't understand all this, and both fight. He left the house many days after the fight, and a year back, he left the village and didn't return. All of them said that he had joined the Naxalites. At home, there were only three *Mem*bers. One was shivering with a high fever, the other was reciting lines from *Bhagavat* and Purana, and *Parabaa* was sitting hungry and thinking about food.

There was hunger, hunger with the break of sleep,

sleep with hunger. Hunger pangs engulfed *Parabaa*, but she was helpless. Sometimes she searched the kitchen to see if anything was left but alas!

Father took his walking stick and went out in that heavy rain. Mother was in pain, and a part of the mud wall was broken. If the other half of the wall breaks, there will be no place for them to stay. Furious wind entered through the broken fence; *Parabaa* was sacred.

After some time, her father returned with empty hands, completely drenched in the rain. *Parabaa* asked: Father, where did you go? You be there at home. I will go to the nearby Rivulet.

Father said: Please don't go.

: I will go and look for some leafy vegetables. If I can find it, then it will be good.

: It's raining heavily. How can you go?

: How did you go?

Her father was silent. It might be raining outside, but there is hunger inside. Father might be expecting that *Parabaa* will be able to make some arrangements. *Parabaa* went outside.

Even a bird wasn't seen outside in that heavy rain, but *Parabaa* went out. The Rivulet was overflowing with rainwater. From where will she get the leafy vegetables? From the neighbours, she learned that the facilities had put their camp in the forest as they couldn't go anywhere due to heavy rain. *Mitrabhanu* said that he had heard firing in the woods.

Parabaa thought that in this time of need, her younger brother was the only person who could help them. He has joined the facilities to help poor people in need. If he learns that they didn't eat anything for six days, he will help them. The forest is close. It's hardly two kilometres. She will meet her younger brother as her elder brother stays in Bhopal. She can't even recognize her elder brother. When *Parabaa* was a child, he visited the village once or twice to meet them. He has changed his religion to Christianity, so the people of her community won't allow him to enter the town.

Parabaa had a good relationship with her younger brother, as they grew up together in poverty. He left everyone and stayed in a foreign country. He is neither in touch with the family nor helps them financially. No one knows if he is alive or dead.

Parabaa goes to meet her brother with a lot of hope without thinking about the wild animals in the forest as if everything is trivial in front of hunger. In *LuiGuda* village, the Naxalites took fifty bags of rice from *Sitani Seth*. What will they do with that rice? They may distribute those among poor people like them. Will fifty bags of rice get over so soon?

Younger brother is in the camp near the village, but why didn't he visit them? Doesn't he want to meet his family? Is it because my younger brother can't come? She has heard that there are so many restrictions there. They do the parade, learn shooting, study, and think about many things. They don't stay in one place for a long time, and if the police come to know about their whereabouts, then they escape. Many girls have already joined the Naxals. If she had joined the Naxals, then who would have taken care of her parents? She has seen how they lament for their children.

When will this war end in the forest? When will they take care of the village like the chieftain? Why are they not closing the liquor shops in the village? Our brothers and neighbours spend most of their time in alcohol intoxication. When she meets her younger brother, she will tell him to stop people from drinking and teach them how to live a life, and after that, he can fight with *Nurusa Alekh Pradhan*.

She will scold him and ask why he joined the Naxal war and forgot his parents? Come with me to the house and see the condition of your parents. Come and see the dilapidated condition of the house. The poor for whom you are fighting don't have anything to eat. Brother, you left the house and parents, but do you ever think about them?

Parabaa had to leave the village on that rainy day, and her fate landed her in hell. *Parabaa* remembers her parents. What will they be eating? How will they be living? There were tears in her eyes thinking about her parents. They must have searched for her everywhere. They might have thought that she got drowned, but her mother always suspected the Muslim boy, so she might have thought that she also eloped with the Muslim boy, like her elder brother. Will her mother ever come to know that *Parabaa* is in Raipur in that hell? Will her father ever stop suspecting the forest guard? Her father is very much annoyed with the forest guard because he had sent her brother *Daaktar* to an unknown place as a bonded labourer.

Parabaa recollected the wicked smile of the forest guard and shivered. She thought she could kill the man if she could get the gun from her younger brother. *Parabaa* was searching for her brother on that rainy day and accidentally met the forest guard in the forest. He was smoking bidi, sitting in his small quarter.

: Who is standing there? He asked.

Parabaa didn't give a reply. They all said that the Naxals were in the forest, but where? They weren't visible as far as she could see.

: Is it *Sarasi*? Why are you here in the forest in this rain? Are you not afraid of your life?

Parabaa was startled. They all say her mother is insane as she searches for her elder brother everywhere. *Parabaa* has tried many times to make her mother understand that her elder brother is in Bhopal along with Baiju Sara's daughter, so why is she searching for him in the forest? Is my brother hiding in the woods for so many years?

Her mother looks at her with wide-open eyes as if she can't connect the present and the past. As if she is still in the world of illusion where there is a dense forest and a wicked witch. *Parabaa* tried to make her understand, but her mother remained in that delusion. As if time is rooted to the spot, she is clutching that.

Parabaa was tired of making her mother understand and finally gave up.

The forest guard was smoking a bidi, and with an umbrella, he came near *Parabaa*. Is that you?

He said: You are *Sarasi*'s daughter, right? Are you mad like your mother? Where are you going in this heavy rain? Come, come to my house.

The wet saree was stuck to *Parabaa*'s body. Her body shivered in embarrassment and fear. She was still and couldn't utter a word, but the man stood before her.

: You are completely drenched. Daughter, please

come, and after the rain subsides a little, you can go. I think you are *Antaraa Satnemi*'s daughter.

She felt a little comfortable when he addressed him as a daughter and was no more scared. She thought the man knew her father and her mother and was speaking to her politely, so why was her father so annoyed with him?

She followed the guard and went and stood on the veranda. She was utterly drenched but couldn't determine how she came so far.

: Where were you going in this heavy rain? Did you run away from home in anger?

: No, why will I be angry?

Parabaa was standing with her head down. She thought if she remained silent, the man would think her mad like her, so she said: There is no rice in the house, so I came to collect some leafy vegetables.

: Do you want to have some rice? The forest guard asked.

On the stove, the rice was boiling. The smell of the rice attracted her as she didn't eat rice for a week, and her mouth was filled with water. She smelled the boiling rice to her heart's content.

The guard held her hand and made her sit on the cot. *Parabaa* shook his hand and said: I am completely drenched.

: So, what. Why are you wearing the wet clothes? Throw it.

Parabaa looked at the man in surprise. He got up and closed the door saying that it was windy. *Parabaa* was scared. Why is the man speaking to remove her wet clothes? Along with the smell of the rice, she could smell something fishy. The old man doesn't have shame. She stood up to free herself from the cage like a deer and said: I want to go home.

He held her shoulder with his hand.: You will go. Will I keep you here? You belong to the village, and if I keep you here, what will people say?

: My parents will be waiting for me.

: Wait. The rice is almost cooked, so have it and go as you have come to my house for the first time. Why is the man so much concerned about her without any reason? They are the untouchable people in the village. People don't allow them to enter their shops and don't drink water from their hands.

The guard said: Today you will eat a plate of rice in my house and go, but what about tomorrow? Won't you feel hungry? Your brothers are selfish as they didn't bother about your parents. If you want, then I can arrange a job for you. Many girls work in the brick kiln at Raipur. You will get seventy-five rupees per day. They will provide you shelter and make arrangements for food. Will you go? You are a girl, so ask your parents. From your village *Bilasini, Jayanti and Tofa* have already gone there.

Parabaa felt as if she was swinging in the air. She felt the man's intention wasn't good, but again, she thought for a while because the man had given job opportunities to many girls. Would she trust the man or not?

The guard touched her bare back and said: Will you go?

Parabaa stood up. To go and not to go is different, but why is the man touching her body?

: I will go home. My parents will be searching for me.

: In this rain? Sit, we will eat together. I don't have anyone here to eat. I cook but don't feel like eating alone and finally throw the food outside. Look at that corner. There is a bag half filled with rice, and rats eat it, so take three to four kilos of rice with you while going home. Look! I am very compassionate, so I am giving you rice but don't tell your father. Someone has instigated your father against me, and he is very annoyed with me.

By then, the guard had almost taken *Parabaa* in his arms, the rice was boiling on the stove, and there was hunger in the stomach. The man was trying his best to seduce her, and there was a foul smell oozing from his body which *Parabaa* couldn't tolerate. She screamed maa maa....

: What happened? I am staying here alone, and you won't understand the pain of a lonely man. Why are you behaving like this?

: Leave me. One had hunger in the stomach, and the other wanted to extinguish the fire of lust. *Parabaa* tried her best, but it was futile. What a dangerous realization is this hunger!

Parabaa was almost half dead, and the guard was wild like a beast. The boiling rice overflowed into the fire; the fire was licking all the white rice; and intermittently, the smell of the chicken curry touched her nose. A wild storm blew away *Parabaa*'s most valuable asset- her virginity. Somebody was looting every pie of her virginity, her womanhood. Leave me, you bastard! For one, life was waning, and for the other, life was completing its turn. One was losing, and the other one was victorious. One had tears in the eyes, and the other had a winning smile on the lips.

Parabaa was wailing like anything. The cry got mingled in the sound of the rain and the crickets of the forest. The smell of the burning rice was everywhere; the burning smell was all around; rice no more looked lucrative to her.

Parabaa got up and came outside, and the forest guard gave her a rat stricken, weevil filled rice bag and said: Take this. Let me know if you want to go to the brick kiln.

Walking home with the bag, *Parabaa* thought, in which forest is my younger brother? Couldn't he hear the cry of *Parabaa*?

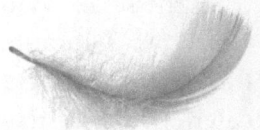

CHAPTER 11

B y then, Pradhan and Saha had a field of ripe corn dotted with flowers that always promised a good harvest. While walking through the bed, the fragrance of the ripe corn brought a sense of contentment. By that time, like a handful of moonlight, The *Kaasha-flower* (Kans Grass) swayed in the breeze on the other side of the *Udanti* River. Herd of Egrets perched on the tree silently like monks, and the treetop looked like a tree loaded with while flowers, and the orange tinge of the sky was dappled by fluffy white clouds that drifted lazily in the gentle breeze.

There was eagerness for the arrival of winter. Towards the end of the night, it was a little cold foot. Throughout the night, with the moist lips, the dew drops smooched the trees, and like the only luxury, most inhabitants were in the arms of sleep, which grew more and more profound.

In this season, there is the hustle and bustle in the forest. The woodcutter, as well as the contractors, take advantage and enter the forest. The forest gets filled with lots of sounds. Someone looks for wood and other stones. People enter the forest for their requirements, and from the other side of the *Udanti* River, one can hear the songs of the stone cutters. Few people, in the name of fate that they never touched or wore, search for precious stones like Rubys and Emerald by deep digging the earth to fetch them from the holes. Within all this, the camps continue, and one hears red salutations. The berries turn red in shame as if they have not seen any of these. Kingfishers dive for their catch, while squirrels and langurs drop partially eaten fruit for the mischief of enjoying the splash and the ripple effect on the clear water, and the berries continue to turn red.

Evening approaches faster, and the village becomes silent more quickly. Elephant herds enter village fields quicker and faster. The haves worry, and those who don't have the areas are at peace.

In Satnemi's ghetto, hunger was at every door front. The same in rains as in winter, sometimes animal bones, and precious stones in another time. Seasons didn't bring a change in their lives.

The Government vehicles and officials visit the village according to their convenience. They ask for the details of the population, from the old people dosing off in hunger. Village roads get stolen, so all village schools, the village well and BPL rice. Young people from the village are robbed, and several young girls recede due to the vanishing act. Still, the government officials don't stop cursing the vices of the cuckoo's porridge. They try to educate them about the harmful effects of grog and instruct them not to sell their children. They distribute malaria tablets, teach about family planning, and finally educate them about eating good food.

Festivals are celebrated one after another. There may need to be more to eat, but *Nuakhai (celebrating new food)* arrives with its grandeur. *Offerings are given to* Goddess *Sureswari* on *Sargi, Mahula* and *bhulia* leaves. For a few hours, one must broom out hunger. After a few hours, hunger arrives at the door in front of the poor with its load of principal and interest. When the crop is infected by pests, the farmer is in trouble, and rituals are still performed for a good harvest with the priest's help. Famine and famine spoil the paddy fields. Time flies between festivals in the game of hope and despair to keep brothers and sons safe (*Pua[8] juintia and Bhai[9] Junintia*). Sometimes the crops are destroyed entirely, and there is famine. Sisters keep fast for their brothers to return home from bonded labour. That year also brother doesn't return to the village, and all fasting and rituals go to waste.

The winter arrives at the village. There were days left for the month of *Margasir*a (December). Days were still there for the spoiled crops. The paddy to mature with fistful smiles. Days were still there to welcome Goddess of Wealth. Days were left to see the dreams. Days were still left for dreams to shatter.

The young girls from the village take the goats for grazing, and instead of *Gharamani*, they are lost. Before dosing off with their toothless mouths, old people don't forget to discuss their youth and happy days. Above all these discussions, the village's thin-legged, beer-bellied, and naked children run after the jeep of Emanuel *Sahib*, Peter *Sahib*, or Gayes *Sahib* without reason.

People in the Satnemi ghetto worry about the young boys leaving the village. If they go, who will carry the

---

8   Pua Juintia- Pua Juintia is celebrated in western Odisha. Mothers across the region pray for their sons' and daughters' long lives and well-being.

9   Bhai Juintia- On the occasion of this festival, girls worship goddess Durga for the prosperity of their brothers.

animal carcass? The old people, with their brown, roughed eyes, looking at the sky, wondering about the imminent danger of their ancestral tradition.

Still, animals die in the nearby villages, and the news reaches the Satnemi ghetto. Reluctant to go, many young boys put their towels on full pants and venture out after drinking liquor from *Kalandar Kisaan*.

No; no, they say,

but again they go to Kalandar's shop to drink.

No; no, they say,

but still, they survive.

Life goes on.

Life goes on.

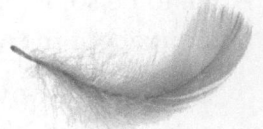

CHAPTER 12

Seeing *Antaraa*, Sarsi got up from the veranda and ran towards him. She said to *Antaraa*: Look! How the man brought me and made me sit in the police station. Sarsi was crying as she spoke to *Antaraa*.

Antaraa was furious when he heard that *Sarasi* was in the police station. There is nothing to eat in the house; in the name of utensils, there is a steal plate and a knife which doesn't have any value. He sent *Nuri Saha* to ask for money, but he refused and told him to mortgage something so that he could give him money. There was a brass pot which *Sarasi* brought from her father's house and is very close to her heart. Even though they needed money, but she never sold it. *Antaraa* didn't feel like mortgaging that, but what was the benefit of going to the police station without cash? Nothing can be done without money.

It was a weekly market day in *Kisinda*. On every weekly market day, *Sarasi* goes to *Kisinda* early and cleans, where *Rehman* sells the goat meat. After that, she takes care of the garden and does other work. *Rehman* sometimes gives her a few pieces of leftover beef meat when she returns. It isn't for those few pieces of meat she goes to *Kisinda*; actually, on the market days, the Murshidabad Muslims come to the market to find out if anyone has old cows at home to be sold and discuss the price. *Sarasi* goes there to find out about the Muslim boy.

Antaraa knows that whenever *Sarasi* goes to the weekly market, she returns drunk. She keeps the rice and mutton near the stove and sleeps. *Antaraa* scolds her and prepares the food. He could understand *Sarasi's* pain. *Sarasi* goes to find out about *Parabaa* but returns disappointed and drinks *Mahula*. *Antaraa* also knows she will feel better if she sleeps for some time. Her young daughter went somewhere, so won't she be worried and in pain? But what is she doing at the police station? Did she find out about the Muslim boy?

Biranchi Bargati lost his bicycle and went to the police station to file an FIR, and there he met *Sarasi*. He informed *Antaraa* that his wife was in the police station. *Biranchi Bargati* is a milkman, and whenever a cow dies in his cattle shed, he tells *Antaraa* to come to take the corpse. In his way, he knows *Antaraa* otherwise; why will he go and inform him about *Sarasi*?

Antaraa was scared when he heard about the police and the police station, and then he asked others to lend him some money. In the ghetto, all are poor like him, then who will lend him money? He went to *Saha* but asked to bring something from home to the mortgage. He couldn't make any arrangements and went to the police station empty-handed.

On the way to the police station, weird thoughts ran through his mind. Did his *Daaktar* come back? Sometimes the police inspector brings back the boys who went outside the village as bonded labourers. Maybe *Sarasi* fought with someone or made a mistake, so she is at the police station. Now his neighbours will gossip about his wife being in the police station. They make up stories about *Sarasi*, and now this incident will be a new addition.

Maybe she might have become a witness somewhere. Doesn't she know that going to the police station means inviting trouble? How can *Sarasi* forget how the police beat him black and blue?

Sarasi held *Antaraa* tightly and cried. Ant ra said: Wait, let me find out what the matter is. *Antaraa* carefully climbed the steps. The constable was standing outside. Ant ra folded his hand in front of him.

: What happened? Asked the constable.

: Sir, you have brought my wife to the police station.

: Is that mad lady your wife? See what she has done to that man. She threw stones at him and injured his head. See how much he is bleeding.

: Sir, she is mad.

Sarasi was surprised and said: Are you also saying that I am mad?

: Why didn't you keep her at home or send her to a mental asylum? The constable said.

: Yes, sir.

: Let her be here for a few days, and then her mind will start working.

: Please don't say that, sir. I have come to take her out of here

: If you say, will I leave her?

: No, sir. Please pity her.

: Even if I pity her, she can't go from here. Did you understand?

Sarasi said: Why did the man push me? I fell to the ground.

Now the man sitting over there said in a mixed language of Urdu and Bengali: Why did you pull me there in the market? How do I know who *Parabaa* is? In the market, you pulled my lungi and disgraced me, and other than that, you scratched me and threw stones at me. Sah b, please don't leave this mad woman.

: Shut up! The constable shouted and said both of you are doing drama here. I will beat both of you then you will realize.

The constable was very busy then as the police inspector was absent. The e will be *Trinath Mela* (A weekend congregation where people smoke Ganja (*Cannabis*) and worship a God with three heads) in the evening. He had told a man to bring *ganja* but didn't return. This is trouble, and he can't earn money. The constable was angry. He said: Both of you go and get money.

The injured man said: Sir, you didn't register my FIR.

Why will the lady complain about you if you didn't do anything? Tell me, where is your house? From where have you come from?

The man said: Why will I take her daughter? Sir, I don't even know the name of her daughter.

: I have a lot of work now. The police inspector will take care of this matter. Sit and wait for him to come.

Antaraa pleaded before the constable and said: Sir, I am a poor person. I don't have money to spend at the police station and court.

: If you don't have the money, then arrange for it. Today there is *Trinath Mela*, so go and put for some cash. I will speak to the police inspector and release your wife from here.

The Muslim boy sitting at a distance was watching this drama. In between, he could understand that he had made a mistake by coming to the police station. The constable will definitely ask him to give him some money. He realized his mistake and wanted to slip out of there. The constable saw him going away stealthily and said: Where are you trying to go? Ras al! You took her daughter, sold her, and pretended you didn't know anything?

I don't know about anything. I was loitering in the market; this old woman saw and troubled me. Lo! How she has injured me.

In between, a man came and handed over a small packet to the constable. He opened the package, smelled it, and kept it in his pocket. Then he looked at both rudely: Get lost from here.

As soon as they heard him, they felt like someone had opened the cage door and were now free. They took a deep breath for being out of this problem. The Muslim boy didn't tell the constable again to write the report, and *Antaraa* put his palm together and bowed his head in front of the constable.

They forgot about their complaint. They were free and ready to leave the police station at the earliest. On the way, *Antaraa* scolded *Sarasi* and said: One day, you will put me in trouble. Who told you to do this? If you were in jail today, then who would have come to help you? Many girls have disappeared from the village. Does anyone go to report in the police station? Are you mad? Do you know what it is to be in the jail? They will beat you so hard that you cannot get up. The constable was a good person. Otherwise, you would have been beaten black and blue. You have made a mistake; how will I show my face to people? People will say that *Antaraa*'s wife was in jail. How much disgrace will you bring to me?

Sarasi wasn't paying attention to what *Antaraa* was saying. Let him say whatever he wants. She was in a different world, engrossed in her thoughts. She was trying to connect the incidents. Did she make a mistake by injuring an innocent man? A long time back, she met *Murrad* when he was laughing and talking to *Parabaa* in the market. She couldn't recollect the exact face of the boy, but there was a black mole on the neck of the man, and *Murrad* also had a black mole on his neck. Who will she ask if the boy is telling the truth or is lying? She felt helpless. After so many days, she came across the boy, but he slipped out of her hands before she could ask him about his daughter. If *Antaraa* hadn't been there with her, she would have followed the man. She would have pleaded with him and said: Please bring my daughter here for once as I haven't seen her for a long time. If the boy leaves *Kisinda*?

Sarasi was in despair, and she regretted her mistake. Though she repented for her mistake, she couldn't open in front of *Antaraa*. She thought that it was because her *Parabaa* left the house. Her daughter was starving, left the house and didn't return. If *Sarasi* had given the money, she saved for *Parabaa*'s marriage for festival food, then *Parabaa* wouldn't have left the house.

Sarasi remembered the day when she wasn't well. One side of the wall was broken, but she didn't have the strength to get up and repair it. The house was flooded with water. It wasn't only the house where the water was flowing, but that flow took away her daughter. Now she is alone as all her children have left her. What is the meaning of this life? For whom will she work now? If they had been the bird's chicks, she would have convinced herself that they would leave the nest as soon as they learned to fly, but they are not the chicks; they are her children.

Sarasi didn't pay any attention towards her husband. She ignored what he was saying. She said: Listen! Our children aren't like the chicks of the bird.

Antaraa was silent. By that time, they have already reached the ghetto. After coming home, *Sarasi* dug the ground and took out a pot. She opened the jar in front of *Antaraa*. *Antaraa* was surprised.

She said: Take this money it will be helpful for some other work. Take this, purchase rice, dal, bhang, and bidi, and go to *Kalandar*. These are all yours from now onwards.

Antaraa didn't eat anything and was hungry. He was not feeling good because of the incident and felt like drinking. His legs were shaky and tired, but he didn't take the money. He thought: This money is from *Parabaa*, and his wife has worked hard to save the money. His eyes were filled with tears. He took his stick, went out and sat on the veranda.

Bhang- A substance that is prepared from the leaves and flower tops of the Indian hemp plant.
* *The Trinath Mela or trinity worship has been practised in different parts of the country following other traditions. But in the eastern region, particularly Odisha, Assam and Tripura.*
* *Ganja - Is the hemp plant when it is used as a drug*

CHAPTER 13

: A dove couple had built their nest on the branches of a tree. Did you understand *Paramaa*?

: They can't stay without each other. Both loved each other. This world is a vicious circle, and everything is an illusion. The dove couple hopped from one branch to the other, sang and danced. So much fun and drama they had locking each other's beaks. After a few days, the hen was pregnant. The cock was happy. The hen laid two eggs after a few days. Both sat on the eggs to hatch. They protected the eggs from the snake, cats, and other animals.

Sarasi was sitting in the courtyard and kneading mud to coat the kitchen wall but was listening to what the people sitting on the veranda were discussing. She knows that though her husband is indolent, but he is knowledgeable. He stayed in *Sonepur* for six to eight months and learnt many things about *Purana* and *Bhagavata*.

On the veranda were sitting *Parama, Kureswar, Jibardhan* and *Chatra*. All of them were of the same age, and *Antaraa* narrated a story from *Bhagavata*, which *Abadhuta* described to King *Jadu*. In between, he sang a few lines for others. *Antaraa* sings well and becomes emotional whenever he speaks about philosophy; his friends usually sit together on their veranda to listen to him.

While listening to him, people from the upper caste laugh and say: See, how much about the *sashtra* this *Chamaara* knows.

Antāraa needed to be in a better mindset. He was thinking about what *Sarasi* had said. She saved money for her daughter with a lot of hope. She also said: Our children aren't like the chicks of the bird. But are they not like the chicks of the bird? Emptying the house, all of them flew away from the nest. *Antaraa* came out to the veranda outside and sang:

> *O king, lend me your ears*
> *a dove in the deep dark jungle*
> *Dwelled in the wilderness*
> *creating a worldly life with his wife.*
> *Never a dull moment*
> *never separating for a moment.*
> *In happy companionship*
> *spent all their time.*
> *They dined and slept together*
> *wandering in the forest.*
> *Whatever she desired*
> *at once the dove arranged.*
> *Like a servant,*
> *he serviced his mistress*
> *As Days passed like this,*
> *the wife got pregnant*
> *After a while,*
> *she laid two eggs.*
> *Fondly the coupled waited,*
> *in hope of a son*
> *Gentle and tender*
> *soon two sons were born*

Parents were happy to see those two beautiful chicks.

Parama said: Even though they are birds, they still love their children. You love your children as you have given birth to them. If Someone dies in the clan, then their family members take him on their shoulders. As such these are their children.

What happened next?

What will happen to the chicks? They slowly developed their wings and fluttered, opened their eyes, and made the parents happy. The dove couple worked very hard to feed their children so that they could grow. Climbing the heights of the sky, they went to distant places to arrange food for their chicks. The mother was worried as she left the chicks alone in the nest. She was apprehensive that someone may fetch them. They were a lot of apprehensions and fear in her mind. Though she may have some food in the beak, her mind was in the nest!

Kureswar said: Do you think that as they are birds, so they don't have any worries?

Chatra said: *Antaraa*, tell us what happened after that. Did the cat eat her chicks?

Antaraa imagined his own four children. Collector, *Daaktar*, Okil and his only daughter *Parabaa*. He imagined his children as the chicks of the dove tottering in the courtyard and picking up the *Mahula* flower, which was kept for drying.

: *Antaraa*, are you sleeping? Clearing his throat and in a rogue voice Parama asked.

: No, *Dada*. I am not sleeping. Now listen to the story about life and living. Will the stomach be filled if you stay at home? The dove couple had to go to many a distant place like we go out searching for the corpse and bones in remote areas. We go to different places, isn't it? From wherever we get the news about animal death, we rush to the place. Have we not gone many places for this?

The hen noticed that her children were learning to fly. They can pass from one branch to another branch. They cannot fly to distant places as they become tired, but they can fly. Their wings were becoming strong, and this age was vulnerable. Children won't understand that there is so much of danger outside. They have big dreams in their little eyes. They said: Mother, see how father can fly so high as if he is touching the sun. He goes around the mountains and the rivers, but can't we fly a little high? They were enthusiastic.

Both of her children flew, returned, and sat near a branch. At that time, a hunter came there. He became greedy when he saw the two beautiful birds. He spread the net and scattered some grains to attract the chicks. The chicks were flying around and singing songs. They didn't know the hunter had spread the net like a drama.

Antaraa said: *Param*, this world is like a net. The more you run after happiness you will get entangled in the net, and there won't be any way to escape. By saying this, *Antaraa* took a deep breath.

His four children also went in search of happiness and didn't return. They got entangled in the pursuit of happiness.

: What happened then? *Chhatra* asked. *Antaraa* was startled, and he sang:

They pecked on the grains
got trapped in the hunter's net.
The coupled returned with food
and with no sight of the children around.
Hovered around the tree and
saw their children, entangled on ground,
In hopelessness and fear
shouting to be saved.
The mother in utter
grief bitterly wailed from her children.
Collapsed onto the ground
and fell into the net.
The husband seeing his wife and children,
in death traps, restrained,
Cried why he should be alive
fainting again and again.

: Aha! Aha, the whole veranda echoed with the words. The dove couple went through so much pain. All of them listening to this, forgot for a while that, with time, they have also lost their children. The only difference is that they didn't see their children losing their life in front of them. That's why there is still a little hope that their children might be living happily somewhere.

Sarasi with clay-stricken hands, ran and came outside, sat, and started lamenting loudly. Where did my *Sanyaasi*, *Daaktar*, Okil and *Parabaa* go? No one was ready for such a situation, as all of them were remorse listening to the story of the birds. As if Sarasi came breaking the rhythm.

Parama said: oh, `daughter in law! You stay silent. Can't you see that we are reading *Purana* and *Bhagavata*? *Antaraa*, what happened to the dove as his children and wife died?

: What can the dove do besides stay alone without his wife and children. He sat on the branch of the tree and lamented.

Chatara requested to recite a few lines about how the dove was in pain.: Tell us how he suffered, how was he reminiscent of his family.

How will I live now
the dove thought to himself?
The universe was against me
the walls of my home have been wreaked.
There is nothing else to live for
there is no more meaning to my life.
My wife, the queen amongst all virtuous wives
devoted and faithful.
Dutifully didn't take a sip of water
until I have had food.
Deserting me alone in this mortal world
she left for her heavenly abode.
Weeping and wailing
he lost all patience.
In despair and grief
flew directly into the net.

The world collapsed in no time. He left his body in deep sorrow while remembering about his family. Saying this *Antaraa* was dumbfounded. No sympathy or empathy for anyone! As if time stopped momentarily and all the listeners were frozen in time. *Antara* got up, took his stick, and walked away from there. Later, everyone left the place one by one for their own houses.

Sarasi ran back from the courtyard and looked around for *Antaraa*. He was nowhere. Where was the man gone after preaching such heavy stuff? Where would he have gone without eating? With the money she took from the pot, she bought ten kilos of rice and kept it in the house. She thought neither curry nor friend vegetables was necessary; boiled rice was enough to fill the stomach.

Sarasi cleaned the stove and lit the fire. She blew on the mouth of the oven to ignite the fire. She was still worried about *Antaraa*. She came outside, looked for him around again and waited for his return. *Sarasi* put rice on the stove. Rice boiled over, and cooking was over, yet there was no sign of *Sanyaasi's* father. Sarasi was worried and disturbed. She felt like crying as worse-to-worse thoughts engulfed her.

She walked towards the rivulet. While she was plucking the leafy vegetables unmindfully, she saw two snails. She took the snails and knotted them in her saree. She thought she would roast and grind them and give *Antaraa* to eat.

Though he left the house in a go, *Antaraa* couldn't decide where to lead to. He was not finding a way out to unleash all his sorrows. He was about to cry but controlled it in front of his neighbours. He left the place, concealing his tears. But who is there for him to go to? For a while, he sat under a pipal tree. On a hot and warm day, the tree had extended its arms like the veil of a mother. The cool breeze made her feel like the mother was swinging a fan for him. There were cuckoos, crows and many other birds who had built nests on the same tree. Chirping a lot, they were flying off and returning to the nest again. A mother and calf were sleeping at a distance, *Antaraa* thought as *Abadhuta* narrated the story to King Jadu. Similarly, Haridas was reading the *Shastra* and *Puraana* and made his disciples understand life's philosophy easily. *Antaraa* felt he should leave this illusionary world and go to the ashram. But is that possible?

Antaraa fell asleep in the lap of mother nature and with the breeze of the mother's fan. When he woke up, it was almost evening. She was so sleeping so long here. Being worried about him, *Sarasi* must be crying at home. She must be searching for him in the village. He thought it was not right on his part to do like this. Slowly he strolled back home.

: Where did you go? Whole of the morning I have been searching for you. Why did you leave me and go? *Sarasi* said and cried.

: Where can I go leaving you? You are my responsibility. With whom will I leave you and go? All of them left us. Where will we go? Can I get free from your illusory clutches, *Sarasi*?

Are you saying that, in the end, I am a burden to you? I was in the police station. I would have died in jail. Why did you bring me from there? Still, you have time. If you want to go, then you can. I won't stop you. You left me and stayed in the *ashram* for a year. People criticized me, but I made these small kids grow up. Who else do I have now? I don't have a son or a daughter. Today I am alive, but tomorrow I mayn't be there. I won't trouble you anymore.

Antaraa understood that *Sarasi* was saying all these as she was hurt. Where can he go leaving this insane lady? Doesn't matter, how much, Avdhoot explained king Jadu, the worldly Illusion will never spare a human.

Sarasi wiped her face and served rice and the dish she prepared by roasting snail and then grinding it with garlic and chillies. Again, the worldly illusion engulfed the dove couple. Despite knowing that everything we perceive is just a grand illusion, there is no way to come out of it- no way out of it.

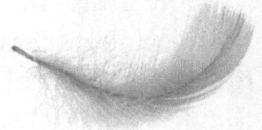

CHAPTER 14

To whom *will Chaiti* complain? After Emanuel *Sahib's* death, *Mem Sahib* stays in Australia. At present, *Agnes Sahib* takes care of everything. He is a good man *Chaiti* doesn't know him well, so she can't muster the courage to meet him. She had told the hostel in charge, Snehalata's sister,: Didi, can you please speak to *Agnes Sahib* to find out the well-being of *Sanyaasi*? We will return to the village after his return. Either we will stay in the village or go to my brother's house.

Sanyaasi had gone for three months, and *Chaiti* was four months pregnant at that time. *Sanyaasi* made her understand that it was a matter of only three months. He also said: *Chaiti*, I will go and earn a lot of money. We will have our own house, and all of us will stay together, including your parents. No one asks for the caste and creed in the city, so we will stay happily here.

Chaiti knows that *Sanyaasi* told all these things just to make her happy. He never thought about money or the family. *Chaiti* knew that he couldn't stay anywhere else other than the Mission. He has tuned himself to the rules and regulations of the Mission so much that he can't stay away from there. It's a lie if he says he will have his own family.

Initially, he wrote letters and sometimes called the

Mission office number. Whenever she heard his voice, she became restless. Every day she drew lines on the wall to keep a count of the day when *Sanyaasi* would return. *Sanyaasi* tried to make her understand over the phone and said: I have entrusted you with two duties. *Chaiti* said: You come back and care for your garden and child. Till I return, take care of that.

: The baby is in your womb. How can I take care of him? You should know how to care for him, so eat appropriately so the baby is born healthy.

Chaiti said: I don't know anything. You come back soon and take care of your child and garden.

: Is that possible? My work is extended for another three months. Can I go leaving my work behind?

Sanyaasi said that he would come back in three months, but it was extended for another three months. *Chaiti* thought that by the time the baby was born, *Sanyaasi* would come back. But time passed; it was now eight months, but *Sanyaasi* didn't come. Earlier, *Sanyaasi* called Snehalata's sister and instructed her to take *Chaiti* for a check-up. She took *Chaiti* to the Mission Hospital. The doctor said that the baby was okay, and she should eat good food.

What good food will she eat? From the day *Sanyaasi* has left, there is no proper time for her to take food. Sometimes she eats, and sometimes she skips it. After completing her daily chores, she used to go to the Mission Garden and work with the gardener for some time. Periodically she cleaned the wild grass or manured the plants. The old gardener insisted she not do any work, to go home and rest as *Sanyaasi* wasn't there.

Chaiti said: He has told me to take care of his child and the garden. The old man laughed and said: Master Babu is a peculiar person. Instead of thinking about the child, he is thinking more about the garden.

: No, uncle. He has told me about two things. To take care of the garden and the child. Sister said he called and told her to take me to the doctor for a check-up.

: Shall I suggest something, something, daughter? As master babu isn't here, why don't you call your mother or mother-in-law to stay with you? Otherwise, if you say, I will leave you in the village.

Whenever *Chaiti* listens to the village or in-laws, she becomes uncomfortable. Still, she could never tell the gardener she had no one other than *Sanyaasi*, as neither her parents nor her in-laws would welcome her. Even if they want to keep her, then also it's not possible.

In the Mission, she is a little bit close to the gardener, so sometimes she speaks to him, but she never talks about her past as she feels uncomfortable.

She was scared as she could feel the child's movement in her stomach. She could understand that the life in her stomach was now ready to see the outside world in a few days but was scared as no one was there with her, and if she died while giving birth, what would happen to the child?

Sanyaasi's silence at that time hurt her a lot. He went for three months but planned to stay there for six months. Doesn't he think about the baby growing in *Chaiti*'s womb? Doesn't he know Emanuel *Sahib* and Marina *Mem Sahib* aren't in the Mission?

For a moment, he suspected him. *Sanyaasi* took photographs of beautiful girls. He stood next to them and took the pictures. Those girls had beautiful skin, black hair, pink lips and beautiful eyes. But after some time again, she forgot about it. She tried to convince herself and thought that her *Sanyaasi* wasn't like that. He could make *Chaiti* fall in love because of music, but will he be able to mesmerize everyone with the theme of his flute? Maybe he should have remembered her as he is busy with his work.

She tried to convince herself, cried and felt helpless. *Chaiti* sits in that small quarter for a long time alone and cries. She remembers the mountain, trees, and river of her village. As she was carrying so, her neighbours sometimes prepared food and gave her sat with her for some time, consoled her and said: Don't worry as we are there. If you need anything, you can call us. Sometimes they say to contact someone from the village.

When she hears about the village, she is in pain. *Chaiti* has her grandfather, her father, her mother, and her neighbours in their own village, but who does Isabella have? For Isabella Satnemi, there is only Christopher Satnemi, but Christopher Satnemi is now in a foreign country and has forgotten her. *Chaiti* cursed Idital.

Bhopal city seems to be unknown to her. The town is more terrifying than the forest. She gets angry with *Sanyaasi*. How can he leave her alone and go? In the closed room, she speaks to herself and feels restless. No one in the Mission belongs to her caste. Most of them are literate, and *Chaiti* feels uncomfortable talking to them. They also don't give so much respect to *Chaiti* and can't adjust to them. After *Sanyaasi* left, the distance has broadened. She feels like going back to the village without anyone's knowledge. Won't her parent's hearts melt when they see their daughter in this condition? Won't they welcome and love their daughter? Still, she couldn't muster her courage when she thinks about her brothers. They may kill her.

She reached the Mission Garden and told the gardener: Uncle, I am petrified. Is master babu fine? There is no phone call or any news from him.

The gardener said: Sister Snehalata was also saying the same thing when I told her about you. She didn't get any information about him. Master Babu doesn't call her. In the office, people also said there was no letter from master babu. He was supposed to come back after three months. But don't worry. He might be on his way, so he didn't write a letter.

When both were talking, *Agnes Sahib* stood near Mother Mary's statue and prayed. The gardener said: Now *Sahib* will come so you can speak to him about your husband. Tell him that your husband was a teacher in this school; he went to a foreign country four months back and didn't return. Ask him: Why is there no information about him?

Agnes Sahib is a good person but different from Emanuel *Sahib*. When he comes to the garden, he tells them when to prune which plant and sometimes works with them.

Agnes Sahib prayed and went back, but *Chaiti* couldn't speak to him. The gardener said: Daughter, if you become so disheartened, then how will you manage? I have to do something for you. Let me see what I can do.

Many times, *Chaiti* has requested Snehalata's sister to help her to speak to Merina *Mem Sahib*. Sister said that she doesn't have her new number and has heard that she no longer stays in Australia.

Chaiti felt as if she has entered the maze. There is no chance of coming out of it, and she finally thinks that things will happen according to her destiny. But what is in her future? Slowly everyone will forget *Sanyaasi*. Then? Now when she goes to the mission hospital, she could feel that the doctor and the nurses aren't bothered about her. No one asked her about her health, nor about master babu, but they used to ask a few days back.

One day along with the gardener, she went to the mission office to enquire about *Sanyaasi*. Instead of giving her information, they troubled her by asking many questions like *Sanyaasi* went for three months, then why didn't he come back till now? How is he? Did he call you? Without informing us, if he extends his stay, then he will be in a problem. That day *Chaiti* heard many more complaints from the office.

The gardener supported her and said: When the Mission has sent master babu outside, then it's the duty of the Mission to know about his well-being, isn't it? If something happens to master babu, won't the Mission be responsible? All of them were silent, listening to the gardener. Then the Head Babu said: *Purandara*, you remain silent. Is there any problem for you? You take care of your work and avoid getting involved.

The gardener became silent, listening to what the *head babu* said.

The *head babu* said: Listen! You can go and ask her. The mission didn't send him. The mission has only sanctioned his leave. *Marina Mem Sahib* has sent him.

There were tears in *Chaiti*'s eyes. She said: Please, let me speak to Merina *Mem Sahib*.

: We don't have her number. She is now staying in Belgium along with her nephew.

There was only darkness everywhere. She felt as if she has become an orphan. Grandfather, why did you forget your granddaughter? Why did you teach me *Idital*? For that, my *Sanyaasi* is lost somewhere.

She touched her womb and said: You are in my womb. Why did you come? If you hadn't been there, I would have been to the village to die.

The gardener was very benevolent. He said: Let's go to the minister. We will plead with him.

: We will go to which minister?

: There is a Scheduled cast and Scheduled tribe minister in your community.

He had studied in this mission and got married here, so this is his house, and how can his family *members* forget him? I won't go. Why should I go?

Finally, *Chaiti* went to meet *Agnes Sahib*. She wasn't scared at all. What can a person do when her family is shattered?

She said: *Sahib*, where did you send my husband that he didn't return? I don't have any information about him. What will I do now?

Agnes Sahib was silent for a while. He couldn't understand what to answer. Then he said: Yes, I have come to know about this. We are trying to find out. We will let you know if we get any information. Rest is up to Lord Jesus.

: Why are you saying this, sir? Why is my *Sanyaasi* not coming back?

: No, no, nothing like that. We are trying. We are trying to find out if there's any problem with the visa. We will inform you. You may go now. We will call you again today.

Where did the man get lost? *Chaiti* said and cried. I don't have anyone other than him. Where will I go?

: Have patience. We don't know if he is alive or … *Agnes Sahib* spoke in English and kept quiet. By God's grace, he didn't talk in Odiya; otherwise, what would have been the condition of *Chaiti*?

Though *Chaiti* didn't understand, she could make out. Whatever is happening with her isn't good. She was highly unwell that day. She had labour pain in the evening. It was excruciating. With the help of the neighbours, she got admitted to the mission hospital. In that pathetic condition, she could hear the flute as if she wanted to cross the *Udanti* river to go to the other side.

Someone said that she gave birth to a baby boy.

Udanti is full of water, and the rocks can't be seen. Though she wishes to jump over the rocks and go to the other side, she is not being able to do so! Still, she could hear the melodious music of the flute echoing in the mountains. After the water subsides from the river, *Sanyaasi* will come to her.

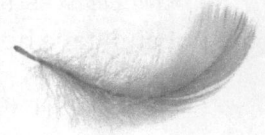

CHAPTER 15

From the dawn, as if someone from within was telling her that the day won't go well. Actually, early in the morning, she woke up with the yowling of a cat – as if a new borne baby was crying.

Yelling at the cat, *Jhumuri* was saying: To my bad luck, you didn't get a place anywhere else other than my house to yowl here right in the morning?

After yowling for some time on the roof, the cat left.

Parabaa was no more feeling slumberous, but what would she do if she got up so early? Though she didn't want to sleep anymore, she didn't get up. At that time, someone knocked at the door.

: Who is that customer who has come so early in the morning? These drunkards are not letting to leave peacefully. *Jhumuri* shouted and slept again. Though *Parabaa* was still scared, she went and opened the door slowly.

: You? She was surprised. You have come here so early. What happened?

: Let's go in. She gave way into the house.

: What happened? You have come so early in the morning? Did anyone tell you anything, dear?

Kundaa was shivering. *Parabaa* brought water from the pot and gave her.

: Drink.

Resisting having, *Kundaa* drank. Though the distance between her and *Parabaa's* shack was less, *Kundaa* was sweating profusely.

Parabaa tried to ease her. Who knows what danger has come upon her? The cat was still yowling.

Kundaa sat silently and said: Sister, your brother had come to my place. Throughout the night, he was in my shack and left just now. On his departure, I have come to you immediately.

Parabaa started shivering. What are you saying, *Kundaa*? Are you telling the truth?

: Why should I lie to you? Don't you trust me?

: No, sister, why shouldn't I trust you? I am not able to believe it. Is it my brother, Okil, who had come?

: Who else, then? Okil had come.

: Did you tell him about me?

: No. I swear, I didn't tell him about you. As you said not to tell anyone, so how can I say?

: Why did my brother come here? How did he get the information? Did you sleep with him without getting married?

Kundaa was surprised as *Parabaa* asked her many questions at a time. They discussed so many things throughout the night, and the time flew. They also discussed *Parabaa* eloping along with the Muslim boy. Both cried. Both cried the whole night. But will *Parabaa* believe that they didn't sleep throughout the night? Why will anyone believe this?

Kundaa said: Sister, do you think your brother was my customer? Can I do that?

: You are my sister-in-law, isn't it? What is marriage for us? What is happiness for us? We make so many people husbands for a night. Do we have any family? Why didn't you elope with my brother?

: I would have eloped, but your brother said: Wait for a few more days as I have some important work, and after that, I will take you from here. You will always stay with me, and I will teach you how to shoot.

: Why? Doesn't he want to get married to you? Why will you hold the gun? Do you think the Antara Satnami clan will be gone? You belong to our caste, so you will get married to my brother. You will take care of my parents, cook, and feed them. Let them get a little bit of happiness at this old age.

: How can I go to the village again? What will all say? They will ask, where was I for so many days? Can I face them?

: What else can we do? Tell me, how did my brother know you are staying here? Who gave him the information? Whoever has given him the information must have also told him about me.

: He should have told me where he got the information. Still, he said: I am like Lord Ramchandra, and I will liberate you from here but not without anyone's knowledge but after killing the Demon.

Parabaa was very scared. The person who gave her brother the information about *Kundaa* won't have told him about *Parabaa*? *Parabaa* goes out rarely. Sometimes she purchases groceries once a week, cooks once daily, and eats them over two days.

Since *Jhumuri* is cooking separately for herself, so, *Parabaa* manages on her own. She works a meal with green chilli and a piece of onion. In the village also, she has yet to get a good meal; what else she can get here. It was true that when she was in the village, there were dreams in her eyes, but her life seemed too long after coming here. She has already forgotten about getting married and having a family. Now she is only bothered about arranging a square meal for herself. She turns blind whenever she thinks about this. She thinks and becomes upset. She doesn't know what will happen when she grows old.

Her brother has come to rescue *Kundaa* from here. Instead of being jealous, she felt happy. It may not be today, but someday she will get married, have a family, and lead a good life. At least the girl will have a good life.

Parabaa said: *Kundaa*, you get married to my brother, and whatever he earns with that, you take care of my parents.

: Yes, sister. Do you think that I will trouble them?

: Listen! *Kundaa*. You don't tell anyone that I am here. I am ill-fated. If I go from here, then who will marry me? I will become a burden for my parents and for you. You promise me you won't tell anyone. *Parabaa* brought *Kundaa's* hand and kept it on her head.

Kundaa was silent.   *Parabaa* said: Go from here and have a happy life.

After *Kundaa* left, *Parabaa* was disheartened. She is now not much friendly with *Jhumuri*. It had been almost a month, but they didn't speak to each other. They are busy with their customers, happiness and sadness and spending their lives in their own ways. There don't help each other even in their time of need.

Jhumuri is very much proud of her beauty. Many people go gaga after her, but that doesn't mean she will disrespect *Parabaa*. *Parabaa* remembered an incident.

Jhumuri said: *Parabaa* can you go to *Kundaa's* house for some time? Is it fair?

: Why do you want me to go? I sit outside whenever your customers are there.

: Don't feel bad about it, *Parabaa*. When my customers see you sitting near the door, they give me lesser money.

Parabaa felt as if someone has given her a tight slap. Disgusting! She thought *Jhumuri* had such a negative notion in her mind for a long time. If she felt this way, why did she take care of her when she came there for the first time? Is it that she showed mercy on her? Is she doing good business now, so there is no more compassion?

Parabaa cried and told everything to *Kundaa*. *Kundaa* said: Why are you crying unnecessarily? Whenever you don't feel good, you can come to me. Her pride will be smashed one day.

Since then, there has been a bit of bitterness between *Jhumuri* and *Parabaa*. *Jhumuri* knowingly hurt her for everything. She tried to find faults with her for little reasons, and finally, they removed the curtain and constructed a wall between the room. *Jhumuri* told the mason building the wall: I will leave within a few days and take a pucca house in *Nepali Basti*.

There are different types of houses in the ghetto. There are different types of rooms. For the Nepali Bengalis, there are separate rooms as they are good-looking and earn well. Their customers aren't those who pay less. Some also go to the houses of *Sahibs* by car when called. They have a fridge, TV, and steel cupboard in their rooms. Few speak Hindi and live a better life though they don't have expensive clothes like the Nepalis. Girls like *Parabaa* do business to earn only twenty-five to fifty rupees to get food. *Parabaa's* condition is still worse because whoever comes says: Why are you lying lifeless? My money is wasted.

When *Kundaa* goes along with her brother, she feels lonely. Why will she live in this hell? *Kundaa* was concerned about her well-being, but let *Kundaa* go.

Parabaa completed her daily chores, had food, and went to the market. She neither took *Kundaa* nor *Jhumuri* along with her. She bought a silver hair clip for *Kundaa* from the saved money. The silver hair clip was beautiful in the plastic box, and she thought she would give it to her sister-in-law, *Kundaa,* to wear during her marriage.

From the market, *Parabaa* went to *Kundaa's* house. *Kundaa* was taking a rest after a meal. *Parabaa* said: I have brought something for you. Look! How is it? I can't attend your wedding, so I bought this for you. She gave the plastic box to *Kundaa*.

Kundaa's felt shy and said: Let your brother come.

She turned pink as if someone from her in-laws' house was visiting them to formalize the marriage.

They both had black tea and discussed life till 4' O clock. *Parabaa* said: I will leave now. The water comes only for ten minutes, and I must fill the water.

After returning from *Kundaa's* house, standing in the queue, *Parabaa* filled water for drinking and kitchen work. After filling the water, she made her bed, combed her hair, washed her face, changed her saree and wore it with a matching blouse. She dabbed powder on her face and applied *kajal*. But she thought she would have looked better without the makeup on her face. But she must do the makeup and sit outside for the customers.

It was bad luck that no customer came to *Parabaa* on that day. *Parabaa* looked here and there and stood in the lane but couldn't get any customers- even not a daily wage earner. She thought that as the cat was yowling early in the morning, it was a bad omen and day for her. In between, *Jhumuri* attended to three customers and had a good income. She was frying fish, and the smell of the fish made *Parabaa* feel hungry.

It was almost 9 O'clock, and as it was winter, it seemed as if it was very late at night. *Jhumuri* had her dinner and went to sleep. *Parabaa* was about to have her dinner when a dark, well-built man came and asked- Are you free?

: Yes. *Parabaa* was happy. If the man pays thirty or forty rupees, then she can manage. Parabaa kept her food aside. After purchasing the silver hair clip for *Kundaa* and paying a hundred and ten rupees, she was left with no money.

She said: Wait. Let me drape a good saree.

: Who has come to look at your saree? Whatever you are wearing, also I will take out now. The man gave a vulgar smile.

Almost two and half times *Parabaa's* weight, the heavily built man came and sat on the cot, and as soon as he sat, there was a cricking sound from the cot. The eyes of the man were red, there was a patch over his lips, and he had a big nose. *Parabaa* isn't beautiful and doesn't pay attention to the look of her customers, but she didn't like the man.

She has seen the man for the first time in the ghetto. Does he belong to this city, as she has never seen him go to anybody's shack?

The man asked: Is your name *Jhumuri*?

Parabaa was silent for some time and then said: No. She is staying in the other half of the house.

: Who are you?

Parabaa didn't give a reply.

: It doesn't matter if you are *Jhumuri* or not.

Come. He said and pulled her towards him. He pounced on her like a vulture, waved a twenty rupee note on her face, and said: This is for your cheeks and started biting her cheeks.

: *Parabaa* screamed.

: Did it hurt you? He asked. He gave the twenty rupee note to *Parabaa* and said: Now it's the turn of your ears. Now tell me about all the parts of your body.

Parabaa was silent.

He said: I will give you money for every part of your body. He took out a twenty rupee note again and said this is for your ears and bit her ear.

Parabaa thought as if she was going to die. She couldn't push the man and go from there. Instead, she was in deep pain. Is the man a human or a beast? Was he a tiger in the disguise of a human being? Why did he come in the middle of the night?

Again, he took out one more note.: Now it is the turn of your nose.

: Leave me. Let me go.

: Why? Don't you like the way I love you? Again, he picked up another twenty rupee note.

Parabaa cried in pain bitterly. From the other side, *Jhumuri* came along with a stick.

: Who, who is that bastard? Rascal! Drunkard! Leave this place immediately. What did you think? Why did you come here, you Demon! Did you come here to eat raw flesh?

The man immediately got up in that half-naked state, looking at the fierce figure of *Jhumuri*. He took the shirt, went out and said: Who is this devil?

: Your mother. *Jhumuri* said and hit him with the stick.

The man whined like a dog and went away from there.

Parabaa looked at *Jhumuri* gratefully, but *Jhumuri* didn't pay any attention. She threw the stick and entered her room, grumbling and saying: To earn money, how can she entertain such customers. God! Please give her good sense.

Though *Jhumuri* was scolding, *Parabaa* still took it lightly. She realizes she isn't alone, and even after *Kundaa* leaves, *Jhumuri* is there.

CHAPTER 16

There was utter silence in the village. People were tongue-tightened. No one came out and said- Let's go and see as if an unknown fear had engulfed the entire place.

But by that time, farmers had already completed the harvesting procedure. Harvested crops were left in the field to dry before further processing. The days were shorter, and the nights were longer. Goddess of wealth had roamed whole of the month of *Margasir (December)* and just returned back. People had their food early, covered themselves with blankets, and slept. The farmers were happy as there was a good harvest, and the common man was delighted as he could arrange food from the scattered grains in the field for a month.

There was no other work in hand or in the fields. There were only stalks left in the areas, and it looked like a beard growing on the face of an adult. As there was no work so people had enough time to play cards. The time passed quickly. In the evening, the villagers gathered in a place, lit the fire, sat around it, and chatted.

There was the smell of jaggery being cooked in *Pradhan's* courtyard. *Pradhan* called the people passing by and gave them a small lump of jaggery. In the fishermen's ghetto, *Sala Ukhuda*[10] was prepared. Spring was searching a route to arrive.

The fog had covered the mountains and forest and had thickly pervaded the atmosphere like a white bedsheet. People groped for their next step and walked cautiously. The guy next to you *also* looked as if he has descended from heaven. The rising sun struggled to come out of the clouds. Slowly the sun peeped out of the horizon, sunrays touched the mountains and trees, and they were uncovered by the misty fog.

Someone had stuck the posters on the wall of *Nurisha's* shop, in the club and in *Sarpanch's* tractor. All were scared as if it was an indication of a disaster. It was as if God in *Kalki*[11] Avatar is likely to arrive with a big sword atop a horse- and a hurricane following him! It was written in the holy book about arrival of these bad days.

Naxal, Naxal. They will attack from everywhere, and the police will follow them. Can anyone hear firing in the forest from the nearby unknown village in the other side of the *Udanti* River? Is it audible? If you listen carefully, you can only hear the silence of the woods. In that silence was hidden a terrible terror. Everyone was gazing at the sky as if red cloud was rising from somewhere!

There was something which was written on the paper stuck to *Nurisha's* shop. The village watchman immediately

---

10 Sala Ukhuda- Fried paddy sweetened by jaggery
11 Kalki- Kalkin, also called Kalki, is the final avatar of Lord Vishnu, who is yet to appear. Kalkin will appear to destroy the wicked and usher in a new age.

ran into the police station. The police inspector came on his motorcycle. Before the sunset, people were inside the house out of fear. Despite all these the day and night were having their cycles. There was no sleep in their eyes, and people stopped playing cards. Nights paved the way for the afternoon and morning found its path crossing the nights- then into the next day! Then after a few days, there was no sight of the police inspector. *Kalki* didn't arrive. Still, the cycle of day and night continued, but there was no work in the fields.

Small kids ran here and there saying Naxal, Naxal though they didn't know the word's exact meaning. But the elderly people could guess many things. The word Naxal wasn't something new for them, but the attack of Naxals in their village was something new for them as it was for the first time.

No one visited *Kalandar*'s liquor shop. He had brought two big plastic containers filled with country rice beer for the *Paush Purnima* (full moon night) celebration. Still, in the middle of the night, someone stuck the posters, and the village people were scared to go.

Whom will *Kalandar* trust? Some of them said that the Naxals would give the poor people land, food and would make their lives happy. Then why did the forest guard tell something else about the Naxals? He also said- Ask them who their leader is? Where does the money go, which they rob from the shopkeepers and the money lenders? If they are your God, then why are you people hungry? Ask, ask those young girls who joined the Naxalites how many of them are virgins? Are the men not exploiting them in the Naxal camp in the forest?

Kalandar was puzzled and felt being in a swirl. The world is like that. Till you have hunger and the mortal body, sin will prevail.

Kalandar bought a lot of rice beer. He thought *Paush Purnima* was ahead, so he would have a good business, as there would be no celebration without rice beer. He was waiting for his customers. Winter had subdued, women from well-to-do families were ready with the ingredients to prepare the delicacies, and children went to ask for *Chher-Chhera* (The young kids go from home to home asking for rice, dal, and friend rice during the *Pausha Purnima* -the biggest festival in western Odisha). Those who were hungry forgot the hunger for a while. In *Kisinda*, the Opera Company had set a camp. People watched opera till the wee hours and returned with dreams of the damsels doing record dance (a vulgar dance in the tune of the movie songs). At that time, someone brought a bit information, and the worried village watchman went to *Kisinda*. Children asking for *Chher-Chhera* forgot to sing the *Chher-Chhera*[12] songs. There was no smell of delicacies being cooked, and the young men forgot to dream of the damsel dancing the record dance. Did the Naxals enter the village?

At the same time, someone gave a news that a dead body was lying in the forest. The person who came and informed was dumb as if he had seen *Kalki (tenth incarnation of Vishnu)*. The police jeep speedily drove towards the forest. Seeing the police vehicle, villagers entered into their houses and locked the doors.

---

12   Chher-cholera -Chhera-Chiara is a unique tradition where village kids ask for sweetmeats and delicacies after the day of Pousha Purnima.

Sarasi was anxious. Her son *Sannyasi* roams in the village, plays the flute, draws images.

Antaraa said: Let *Kalki* come. *Kali Yuga* will end and usher in the new epoch of Satya Yuga. All the sinners will die, and the pious people will survive. This will be the beginning of the age of truth.

The police jeep returned from the forest after two hours. The policemen combed the woods for two hours and finally returned to the village. The police jeep stopped on the middle of the village road, and a few policemen jumped out. Two policemen brought a dead body and threw it down as if they had gone hunting for a deer or sambar deer. The body fell on the ground with a thud. The driver started honking the horn, and slowly, the villagers opened the door of their hamlets. They stepped out of their homes in fear; stood on the verandas of their houses and saw a dead body on the ground. The dead body's eyes were open, looking towards the sky. Its mouth was open, had mud and dust all over the body and dry blood stains on the vest.

Police shouted: Identify him. Whose son is he? Is he the boy from your village or not?

The onlookers were shivering with fear. Who will go and answer the police? Someone ran and informed *Antaraa*.

: *Antaraa*, run quickly and see your son.

: Who, which son? *Daaktar*? Did he come back? Where is he?

: You come along with me. They have brought your son from the forest.

Sarasi was cleaning the utensils. She heard and said:

What did you say? She came to the veranda and asked: Who has brought my son from the forest? Where did my *Sanyaasi* go? *Sarasi* ran after the man. *Antaraa* was walking behind, and *Sarasi* was running ahead insanely.

Sarasi was crying- My *Sanyaasi*, my *Sanyaasi*. Why were you hiding in the forest for such a long time?

Sarasi saw that there was a dead body on the ground. She came and saw that the police jeep was standing on the village road and people surrounded the body. When they saw her, they gave her way. She was dumbstruck for a while.

Her Okil wasn't looking at his mother. He was looking towards the sky with open eyes. Her son Okil was very stubborn and adamant. Blood had clotted near his chest, and his body was smeared with mud and dust. Who killed him so brutally? What did he have for which someone killed him?

Sarasi ran and cleaned the dust from her son's body and cried bitterly. After a long time, *Sarasi* could see one of her children. Okil had grown a beard and moustache. Her son has grown up. *Sarasi* held her son tightly.

Antaraa stood there still. He felt as if Okil was saying to him- You didn't love me, father, so don't be sad for me.

Antaraa said in a feeble voice: How can't I be sad? You left me alone.

Police asked *Antaraa*: Is he your son?

: Yes, sir.

: Did your son join the Naxals?

Antaraa was silent.

Police said: He had come to kill the forest guard. Go and sit in the police jeep.

The police jeep left the place along with the dead body of Okil. *Sarasi* sat there silently. Tears rolled down from her eyes. Slowly people left their homes and closed their doors. There was silence and silence everywhere. The whole village was shivering.

■ ■

Black Eagle Books

www.blackeaglebooks.org
info@blackeaglebooks.org

Black Eagle Books, an independent publisher, was founded
as a nonprofit organization in April, 2019. It is our mission
to connect and engage the Indian diaspora and the world at
large with the best of works of world literature published
on a collaborative platform, with special emphasis on
foregrounding Contemporary Classics and New Writing.

www.ingramcontent.com/pod-product-compliance
Lightning Source LLC
Chambersburg PA
CBHW020154120726
47903CB00007B/2546